S0-DYA-642

# SECRET

# LIFE

# OF

# GUYS

SPECIAL THANKS TO J.H. CARROLL,
ALFONSO RYAN NERZ, JASON
ALTMAN, AND MICHAEL FITZGERALD
FOR ALL THEIR HELP.

ISBN 0-439-11468-3

Distributed under license from
The Petersen Publishing Company, L.L.C.
Copyright © 2001 The Petersen Publishing
Company, L.L.C. All rights reserved.
Published by Scholastic Inc.

Produced by 17th Street Productions,
an Alloy Online, Inc. company
33 West 17th Street
New York, NY 10011

Teen is a trademark of Petersen
Publishing Company, L.L.C.

12 11 10 9 8 7 6 5 4 3 2        3 4 5 6 7/0

Printed in the U.S.A.        01
First Scholastic Printing, April 2001

# SECRET

# LIFE

# OF

# GUYS

SCHOLASTIC INC.

New York  Toronto  London  Auckland  Sydney
Mexico City  New Delhi  Hong Kong

THERE'S A REASON MY NAME'S NOT ON THE COVER OF THIS BOOK.

AND NO, IT'S NOT BECAUSE MY PARENTS STUCK ME WITH ONE OF THOSE WINNERS LIKE "HERMAN HERMANSON." THE DEAL IS, IF I'M GOING TO GIVE UP ALL THIS INSIDE INFO ON THE MALE MIND, THERE'S NO WAY I CAN MAKE MY TRUE IDENTITY KNOWN TO THE WORLD. IF WORD GOT OUT, I'D BE TOAST! BESIDES, I COULD NEVER LOOK A FELLOW GUY IN THE EYE AGAIN AFTER ADMITTING WHAT WE SAY ABOUT YOU WHEN YOU'RE NOT AROUND AND THAT YES—WE DO CRY (SOMETIMES

OVER YOU!). BUT YOU KNOW WHAT? I FIGURED SOMEONE HAD TO BREAK THE SILENCE BETWEEN US.

So HERE IS THE ABSOLUTE TRUTH, DISCOVERED THROUGH A CAREFUL EXAMINATION OF MY OWN (BE KIND!) PAST, CONVERSATIONS WITH MY FRIENDS, AND INTERVIEWS WITH A BUNCH OF BRAVE GUYS AND THEIR (EVEN BRAVER!) GIRLFRIENDS. OF COURSE, IT'S IMPOSSIBLE TO CAPTURE THE THOUGHTS AND OPINIONS OF ABSOLUTELY EVERY SINGLE GUY, BUT THIS COMES PRETTY CLOSE, IF I DO SAY SO MYSELF. I PROMISE TO GIVE YOU A ROAD MAP TO OUR MINDS, EXPLAINING WHAT MATTERS MOST TO US AND WHY WE ACT THE WAY WE DO. THE REST IS UP TO YOU.

L. A.

# INTRODUCTION

What's the deal with guys, anyway? We can go from annoying to charming, disgusting to sweet—with little or no warning. In fact, if guys are from Mars, you probably wish we would go back there once in a while just to make your lives a little easier.

Well, this book gives you the lowdown on what goes on in our heads and what we really think about you! Learn what excites us, what makes us mad, why we get so jealous—and maybe, for once, how to get us to stop thinking about ourselves and open up a little!

But first, be prepared—if you really want the truth, then you'll have to dig through our closets and our lockers and even spend some time in our brains. But luckily, there is a reward! Find out what we really think about the way you wear your hair. Why we're afraid to ask you out. What we look for in girls, and what turns us away.

The truth is, when you break it down, we're actually pretty simple creatures. Learn a couple of basic pointers—and I mean basic—and you will quickly realize that we're not that scary after all.

# CHAPTER ONE:

# BEHIND CLOSED DOORS

To really understand how we think, you have to spend a little time inside our world. That includes our messy bedrooms, our sweaty locker rooms, and our family dinner tables. It even means listening in on a session of guy talk. . . .

## Boys Will Be Boys

What do we talk about when you're not around? Wouldn't you like to know? Sorry, I can't tell you everything. All right, if you insist . . .

First off—and I'm guessing this won't come as a huge shock—there's sports. We can go on and on about what makes Shaquille O'Neal unstoppable, why the New York Rangers are struggling, and the unbelievable highlights we saw last night on ESPN's SportsCenter. If we're athletes ourselves, we can analyze (and reanalyze) every amazing play we made in our game yesterday. We can even talk about sports video games.

I've had a lot of girls go off on me about the way we can ramble on about sports. But see, it's just as weird to us that you can sit on the phone for hours and talk about who did what at school today. What really amazes us is that it's no problem for you to talk about "feelings" as easily as you ask your dad to pass the salt.

The bottom line? Sports are a safe way for us to accomplish what you do when you have those long conversations with your friends. There's nothing personal involved, so we don't have to feel like we're revealing anything too deep or even that meaningful. But it's still the way we stay connected. My friend Mike and I watch the World Series together every year, no matter what.

And during the commercial breaks, while we sit there debating whether the pitcher has anything left in his arm, we're bonding in our own way.

So what about when we're not busy analyzing the latest play-off game? Well, we make fun of each other. A lot. We have tons of inside jokes, obnoxious nicknames, and made-up words (more on this later) that send us into fits of laughter but would probably only bore or confuse you. Yes, we can actually spend an entire afternoon finding new ways to twist each other's last names into insults. I still remember how excited my friend Jason got when this new kid started hanging around us freshman year—Diego Trachenbergenstein. Go figure.

So, sports and jokes. Hmmm, let's see. What else? Oh yeah, we talk about you. Yes, the topic of girls never gets old. This conversation usually begins with questions like, "Did you see Robin at the football game? She looked so hot." Or it could start with a teasing jab, like, "You're into Robin, aren't you, Steve? Come on, admit it." (This is followed by a flurry of, "Yeah, you are!" and, "Come on, Steve, admit it!") Quick pointer—since we do talk about you a lot, it's a good move to be your usual cool self to your crush's friends. The last thing you want is for him to bring up your name, only to hear his friends rip into you. (Unless, of course, his friends are mean, nasty people . . .)

Another thing: Yes, we do talk about your looks a lot. Don't you talk about cute guys with your friends? I would love to say that we have in-depth discussions about your personalities, right before we discuss the meaning of life. But the closest we come to that is comments like: "You should go for her, man, I think she's one of the coolest girls in our class. Forget Isabel White. She only goes out with seniors, anyway."

So . . . sports, stupid jokes, and girls. Pretty harmless, right? I told you we aren't all that complicated.

## GONE IN SIXTY SECONDS

It's no secret that we have shorter attention spans than you. We get distracted easily, and boredom comes fast. One week we can be totally into basketball, busting out NBA gear and bringing a ball to school. Then suddenly we must own every X-Men comic. It doesn't mean we're all total flakes—just that we like to try new and different things.

My friend Eddie is an extreme example. Every two weeks—literally—the guy has a new hobby. If he's not trying to nail down the highest score on Tetris, Eddie is memorizing all of Adam Sandler's movie lines. Not that he's succeeded at any of this, but that's not the point. For a two-week stretch all Eddie can focus on is the newest thing. Eddie's girlfriend, Nicole, admitted to me that it drives her crazy sometimes trying to keep up. She feels like she's supposed to be just as excited about all of his latest crazes in order to stay involved in his world.

The truth? She doesn't have to be, and neither do you. We get that you're not always going to want to come along for the ride, and that's fine. So don't worry about getting whiplash attempting to understand your guy's obsession with astronomy when he's already moved on to rock climbing. You can ask a few questions or let him babble to you about which planet has the hottest temperature. (See, Mercury is the closest to the sun, but Venus actually has the hottest surface because of its greenhouse effect. . . . Oops, uh, okay. Yeah, I went through my own astronomy phase.) But you certainly don't have to go out and buy yourself a telescope!

Oh, and here's an extra hint if you want to keep from getting your feelings seriously hurt at gift-giving time—you might want to avoid buying him something connected with his current hobby of the moment. If he's over it in a few weeks, your gift will end up in the closet and you'll probably go and take it all personally (we wish you wouldn't do that so much!). Instead, try to figure out which hobbies are here to stay. Even a guy with the attention span of a gnat, like Eddie, sticks with certain things. He hasn't lost interest in his baseball card collection—that 1975 set's almost complete. And he's still dating Nicole.

## Boys' Toys

There's this crazy idea out there that we're obsessed with video games. Ha! Wait—what did you say? Your brother has the latest version of Tomb Raider? I'll be right back . . .

Okay, so it's true. Most of us are totally, completely obsessed with this stuff—from N-64 to Dreamcast to Gameboy to good old computer games. Here's the thing: You have to remember that we're competitive freaks. There's a lot of pressure on us to win, win, win. But it's not always easy being a star on the basketball court or football field. So, video games give the rest of us a chance for victory.

Even though my friend Jake says that he hasn't played Mortal Kombat in three years, every time he sees our other friend Gil, they "debate" the issue of who had a higher score. After all this time, a hundred points is still a big deal.

So the next time you ask a guy if he's into video games and he shrugs and says, "Nah, whatever," real-ize that it's totally possible that he just doesn't want you to know the truth about his habit. And if he admits it, maybe you should keep in mind everything I've just told you before you give him a hard time about it.

## PLAY BALL!

My friends and I love to watch sports. No, we're not the kind of fans who splash paint on our faces and scream at TV sets (even though I've hung out with those guys before, and they're pretty fun!). Still, if a big game is on, don't even bother making plans with us.

Some girls love sports as much as we do. My ex-girlfriend Kristin was totally into basketball—probably even more than I was. Now, she screamed at the TV. But in general, this is one of those big hot button issues between our genders. Many of you just don't get why it's such a big deal to us to watch the important (and okay, sometimes not so important) games.

Here's a suggestion for all you antisports girls— watch a game with us every once in a while. You might actually think it's cool, and if you don't know what's going on, why not let us explain the rules to you? We love feeling like we're teaching you something new, and there's nothing that can pump up a guy's self-esteem more than being able to spout off sports rules and facts like an expert. You don't have to high-five us at the final buzzer if you don't want. But if you could force an, "Ooh, that was nice," or, "God, they're animals!" or something similar, we'll be pretty pumped. Oh, and you might actually find it entertaining. I swear.

Chris, 17—one of the first guys I interviewed—is the sports editor of his high school paper. He loves all types of sports, from fly-fishing to football. When he started dating April, this quickly became a problem. She's an actress and a dancer and in great shape. But she couldn't understand Chris's obsession with just watching other people play sports.

One day Chris was heading down to the varsity football field to cover a play-off game. He wasn't planning on bringing April with him since he knew that she thought the games were beyond boring. But then he had an idea of how to change her mind. Instead of inviting April to go to the football game, Chris told April she should check out the cheerleading squad. He figured that as a dancer, she would take the bait.

It worked. When they got to the game, Chris started off by talking to April about the cheerleaders, which gave her an opening to share some things about dancing. Then, since April realized that Chris was really making an effort, she asked him a few questions about the football game. Chris went off about why this game was so important, what was happening on the field, what should be happening—you know, the usual. By the end of the game April was standing up and screaming for the team, even though she wasn't sure why.

Chris loved the fact that April was finally giving his world a chance. "I liked April a lot before that game," he told me, "but ever since that day it's been even better. She really tried to understand what was going on out there and why it mattered so much to me. Seeing her cheer was the best feeling."

The way April tells it, it was more about figuring out Chris than understanding the game. "Chris always gets so intense whenever sports comes up," she explained. "I wasn't sure why, but now that I've seen him in his sportscaster mode, I think it's a lot like how being onstage is for me. It gives him confidence, and it's where he feels like he belongs."

Bringing April to the game was a smart move for Chris, and it ended up making their relationship stronger. But mostly that's because April handled the whole thing so well. She agreed to come with him instead of throwing a big fit about how boring it would be, and then once she was there, she let him be his natural self. In other words, she gave it a chance— which is a bigger deal to us than you may realize. Just trying to understand something that's important to us will prove that you care. And then you have every right to expect us to return the favor.

The sports dilemma doesn't always work out this

smoothly, though. A friend of mine, Jonah, is so obsessed with televised sporting events that he won't sacrifice them . . . for anything. But instead of admitting that he's staying home for an NBA play-off game, a hockey game, or a tennis match between Serena and Venus Williams, Jonah tries to slip out of dates with stupid excuses or by just stuttering something lame like, "Uh, I have to go now," and then bolting.

Jonah knows that a lot of girls will get pretty ticked off if he says that a Mets-Yankees game takes priority over hanging out with them. So he dodges questions, plays superevasive guy, and always ends up losing the girl, anyway—because they think he's hiding something much worse than a love of sports or that he just doesn't want to spend time with them.

A few months ago Jonah started dating Debi, a seriously cute girl. He really liked her, and he didn't want to mess it up. So he came to me for advice, and I told him he should just tell her that it's a big deal for him to watch sports. Maybe she'd even want to come watch them with him.

Well, Jonah tried it, and unfortunately it blew up in his face. She had the exact reaction he'd been afraid of—she couldn't believe he really wanted to spend that many Friday nights sitting home watching TV. They broke up soon afterward.

# THE
# WRESTLING THING
(FOR THOSE OF US WHO ARE DRAWN TO THIS
ADMITTEDLY BARBARIC FORM OF ENTERTAINMENT)

There's actually a simple explanation for the lure of a good wrestling match—it helps us deal with the pressure from school, parents, friends—and yeah, girls. Sometimes we get stressed out enough to actually climb into a ring and break a chair over someone's head. But we don't have to because guys like Stone Cold Steve Austin do it for us.

Plus if you've ever watched wrestling, you know that it isn't all about big muscley people beating each other up. Okay, yeah, that's a major part of it—but now there are little stories that go along with all the fighting. We could never admit to watching a soap opera, but some of us do enjoy those twisted dramatic plots, and wrestling shows give us a chance to watch them without feeling silly.

Another thing—just because we might watch wrestling a lot on TV doesn't mean we're going to go around giving everybody who crosses our path full nelsons. If you do see some guys tackling each other and faking fancy moves, you should know we're just playing around.

Wrestling is essentially harmless because you won't have to worry about your guy spending all his time screaming at a ring instead of being with you. Why? Because for most of us, after about five body slams, three arm twists, and a pile driver, the sport gets repetitive and boring. That's when our minds start drifting a bit—remember, we have short attention spans—and all of a sudden we're wondering what you've been doing the whole night. . . .

Not all guys are as extreme as Jonah. But if the one you're dating is and if you, like Debi, can't stand the idea of being with someone chained to ESPN, that's your choice. You should never settle for less than what will make you happy. But you might feel differently if you take a little time to understand why sports (or any other obsession your boyfriend has) matters so much—like April did. I promise it will be worth it.

Why are we such freaks about anything with a ball and a crowd? Maybe it's because we're born with this bizarre need for battle and competition, and since there are presently no world wars to attend to, we get our aggressions out on the sports field and the almighty couch. Maybe. I don't have time to figure it out right now. The football game just started!

## No Trespassing

Let's talk about personal space. For starters, we love our bedrooms. It's the one private place where we can chill out and be ourselves. It's almost like the secret forts we used to build when we were kids, only bigger and more loaded down with our junk. Parents, siblings, and strangers are definitely off-limits.

This doesn't mean we won't let any of you in our rooms. Just be warned—there may be a major mess on the floor, with T-shirts hanging off the backs of chairs and books upside down on the carpet. But that's all part of our bizarre system. We like to think of it as organized chaos. Beneath the pile of T-shirts is our English paper. Somewhere in that desktop of baseball cards, video game cartridges, and CDs could be a note we wrote to you and were afraid to send because it was too cheesy.

If you can handle the mess, you'll find that our bedrooms reveal a lot about us. What kind of books and music do we like? Do we have Limp Bizkit posters, pin-ups of Michael Jordan, or artwork on our walls? Did you notice the picture of our family or the soccer trophies in the cabinet? We want you to be interested in what we do. Feel free to ask questions. We'll tell you why we think Michael Jordan rules or why he's suddenly so annoying since he retired. Maybe we'll even tell you why we're closer to one sibling than the others.

Maybe. At the same time, be careful not to overstep the boundaries. Our rooms are filled with embarrassing stuff—often things we'd rather not talk about. We don't want you to see our dirty underwear or flip through the pages of our old yearbooks filled with notes from ex-girlfriends. We might just feel weird that a relative stranger—a girl, no less—has invaded our fort.

My friend Dan had a thing about his room—he wouldn't let anyone inside it. I mean anyone. I got a glimpse once, once, on the way to the bathroom, and the place looked like an abandoned building after a tornado. Disaster. Clothes draped over the lamps. Cheetos wrappers on the ground. Speed metal music blasting from his speakers.

Anyway, Dan started dating this really cute girl, Jen, our junior year. Let's just say he was in deep like with Jen, the kind where you smile all the time in that super-dopey way. "Are you going to show Jen the pit?" we teased him. He got so nervous whenever we brought it up, just imagining that Jen, a total neat freak, would see his mine shaft of a room and break up with him. Eventually Jen started to get frustrated that Dan wouldn't show her his room. He'd seen hers, after all. What was he hiding? She kept thinking that he was holding back from her or something, like there was another girlfriend hiding in the closet. (Side note—you girls have got to learn to take things less personally. It's usually about us, not you. Really. Guys are definitely the most self-centered creatures in the universe—which I will get in huge trouble for admitting, but it's true.) Eventually Jen stopped pressuring Dan to see his room, which was a good move since it's never fun to have someone nag you like that. But she also started pulling away from him. You know, not calling him back as quickly as she used to, sending shorter e-mails. The usual stuff.

# FIVE THINGS
## YOU WON'T FIND
### IN HIS ROOM
(AS LONG AS YOU STAY CLEAR OF THE CLOSET)

1. Stuffed animals
2. Pajamas with patterns on them
3. Themed bed and/or sheets (like Star Wars sheets or a race-car-shaped bed)
4. Anything his mom made for him
5. Dorky pictures of him (like the one when he was five, wearing one of those turtlenecks with little turtles all over it)

Well, Dan bugged out. This was it. Game over. He couldn't lose Jen over a stupid messy room. So he invited her over. When Jen got there, Dan was shaking, but she just strolled in, sat down, and actually smiled. She said his room "looks like a piece of art, just like I expected." Dan was shocked at how cool Jen was. He searched through a big pile of laundry for his guitar and played a song for her.

So, what can you learn from Jen? First of all, understand that being invited in is a big deal, even for those of us whose bedrooms don't resemble natural disasters the way Dan's did. If we don't ask you over right away, it's probably not because we don't like or trust you enough. It's just that we care what you think of us more than you realize, and we have this image in our minds of you running screaming from our rooms without looking back.

And if you do get the green light about entering our rooms, then take a clue from Jen and act like it's a palace, even if that's not really true. If you step inside and immediately wrinkle your nose, all you've done is confirm our worst fears. Don't expect a return trip.

## Party Time

I don't know what it is, but parties do strange things to guys. In the die-hard pursuit of fun, some of us laugh ourselves into the ground, embarrass everyone around us, and flirt with every girl we run into. Others of us hide in the corner, acting like we grew up in the wild with only gorillas for companionship. Can you say social skills?

And that's just when we go by ourselves. When we show up at a party with our girlfriends, it's even worse. So many questions that we can never answer. If someone hits on you, what are we supposed to do? Beat him up? Ignore it? Pull you away? And what if a really cute, sweet girl we've never seen before starts flirting with us? Should we tell her we have a girlfriend, or is that obnoxious? Maybe we should flirt back, just a little.

Flirting is harmless, right? But what if you notice? Do we need to apologize?

My friend Nicky still remembers the night that almost ended his relationship with Ann. They'd been going out for about three months, and things were getting serious. They talked every night on the phone before bedtime, left notes in each other's backpacks, that kind of thing. Then came Jed's end-of-school pool party. Nicky and Ann went to different schools, and it was the first time she'd gone somewhere with a lot of people from his school. Right after they arrived, Nicky ran into two guys from the lacrosse team who insisted on going through another play-by-play of their huge comeback win the week before.

As soon as Nicky saw his friends, he let go of Ann's hand. He says it was an instinctive thing, like dodging a speeding car. All he could imagine in that split second was the way the guys would tease him later. "Man, you're so whipped," and all that. But Nicky took it a step further—he didn't even introduce Ann to his friends. He stood there rehashing the plays with his teammates while Ann got increasingly annoyed.

This is a common complaint from girls, and we know it. But unfortunately, it's practically irresistible for us to try and act macho around groups of guys. That's because when we're alone with those guys, they're going to give us a lot of grief that we don't want to deal with. You're not around for that, so you think we're being silly. But imagine it was the other way around. Would you want to be the joke of all of your friends? There's a lot of pressure from other guys for us to not only act tough but also to seem "in control." We're so afraid of looking like we're leashed to our girlfriends that sometimes we go overboard by almost ignoring them.

It didn't take Nicky long to pick up on the angry-girl vibes coming from Ann, and he quickly made an excuse to get away from his friends, then spent a major part of the night apologizing. When she pointed out that he'd acted like she wasn't even standing there, he realized that he really had gone too far, and he made sure to introduce her to anyone else they ran into that night. See, he really did care about Ann and was truly oblivious to how much he had hurt her. So go easy on your guy if he pulls a Nicky and messes up like that. As long as he shapes up a little, you can trust that he's trying. Although if we do go too far and do something stupid or disrespectful, don't put up with it. The pressures of group situations make us do strange things because we feel like our reputation is on the line. But it's still not fair to you.

## Family Circus

Yeah, it's true—some of us have a tough time letting you get close to our families. The biggest reason is definitely the embarrassment factor. I mean, what if my mom decides to bring up her favorite story about when I was four and completed a front-yard hundred-meter dash dressed in my tighty whities?

Mom also might pull out some baby pictures while you're over. Aw, how cute. There's me, nude in the sandbox. And there's me with my little sister, dressed up as two M&M's on Halloween.

One of the guys I talked to, a 16-year-old named Mike, gave me a perfect example of why he likes to keep his mom off-limits to girls. The first time Mike's girlfriend, Chandra, came over for dinner, Mike's mother asked Chandra (while passing the pot roast) if she'd had a chance to see Mike's trophy from the Little Tike Bowling Contest he'd won in third grade. Mike's mom thought it was such an amusing little story, and so did Chandra, who almost spit up a mouthful of peas. Mike, on the other hand, wouldn't have chosen his childhood bowling exploits as the numero uno way to impress Chandra with his manliness. Suddenly the pot roast didn't taste as good as it usually did.

Dads can be even worse. My friend Rick's dad still

calls him by his childhood nickname "Dickie" every time guests are over, including his girlfriends! My own dad has been known to pull the silent treatment to intimidate first-time visitors. My first girlfriend, Amanda, was convinced my dad hated her for the longest time.

And that's just parents! Siblings can be a touchy area, too. Brothers (both older and younger) love any chance to tease us mercilessly. "What is she, your girl-friend?" they'll ask. We worry that they'll ask us annoying questions like whether we've kissed you or not. Sisters don't make fun of us as much, and in fact, there isn't usually as high a risk of mortification. But sisters are still dangerous territory because of the pos-sible friendship factor.

Josh, 18, told me all about his own personal sister nightmare. His ex-girlfriend, Judy, was the same age as his younger sister, Sarah. After Judy had gotten to know Josh's family a little, Judy and Sarah hit it off and became friends. At first they would just chat on the phone for a few minutes when Judy called for Josh. But before long Josh would come home from football prac-tice and see Judy hanging out in the living room with Sarah, watching TV together.

This bugged Josh for several reasons. First, he wanted Judy to come over to see him, not his sister.

When it comes down to it, we're possessive creatures. Josh couldn't understand why his girlfriend suddenly seemed closer to his own sister than to him. Plus now Judy could show up at his house even when he wasn't the one who'd invited her. His personal space was gone, just like that. Seeing each other seemed less special because she was always hanging around his house.

So what did Josh do? Well, being a guy, his reaction wasn't exactly the most mature one in the history of time. Okay, so it was pretty immature, but give the guy a break, will you? Anyway, Josh started making fun of Sarah when Judy was around, the way he used to do when they were little kids. "I know it was stupid," Josh mumbled to me, with the appropriate shade of red on his cheeks. "But I was desperate to find a way to make Judy stop liking Sarah so much!"

Of course, the "plan" backfired. Judy defended his sister, telling Josh that she thought it was terrible he would treat Sarah that way. Josh and Judy ended up getting into a huge fight and eventually broke up over this.

So now Josh no longer had a sister and a girlfriend who were close friends. Instead he had a sister and an ex-girlfriend who were really tight! Finally Josh admitted to Sarah that her friendship with Judy was kind of rough on him, especially because he didn't want to hear the day-by-day details of Judy's new dating life. They made a deal where Sarah would hang out with Judy outside the house, at least until more time had passed since the painful breakup.

You're probably sitting there thinking that Josh was a jerk, anyway, and the whole thing was his fault for not coming clean in the beginning. Yeah, you've got a point, but the thing is, it's hard to be honest about stuff like this. Sometimes the guy won't be able to, so it's up to you (since I am, after all, giving away the secrets of the other side!) to try and be aware of how he might be feeling. It's okay to get to know his family, even to become close to them, but be sure to make it clear to your guy that he's the reason you're there, not any of his relatives. And if you notice him suddenly acting sullen and childish when you're gabbing with his sis, mom, pet goldfish, etc. (à la Josh), call him on it. Ask him what's up, and find out if there's a way you can keep the relationship with his family without hurting the one you have with him.

In the long run, it's not always a bad idea to keep a little distance from the fam, anyway, especially at the beginning. There's nothing worse than breaking up with someone and feeling like you're breaking up with their whole family, too. I remember the summer when I was dating Meg, her parents invited me to go to the beach one weekend. I was psyched for the chance to go away, and I thought they were pretty chill for parents, so I said yes. It was a really great day—bright sun, excellent waves. Her parents spent all this money on me for lunch, and they even bought me a pair of sunglasses because I had forgotten mine.

Well, about a week later Meg and I decided to call it quits, and I was wrecked. It was bad enough we weren't seeing each other anymore. But I felt like I had to explain the reasons to her parents since they had been so nice. I even thought I should mail back the sunglasses.

So basically, here's the deal: We don't want our parents to scare you away or for you to like our siblings better than you like us. We're afraid of those icky, awkward emotional situations that come when we get too close to people we'll have to stop seeing. You've probably had to deal with that before, too—so I bet you know exactly what I'm talking about. That doesn't mean you won't ever gain access to our worlds, but it won't happen overnight. And it goes both ways—don't expect us to sink right into a groove with your family. It takes a while for guys to strip off the armor for you, not to mention your parents and sisters and brothers!

## Talking the Talk

In general, we're not a wordy gender. Shocker, right? Especially when "relationship stuff" and "feelings" come up, our instinct is to run for cover. We just don't see the point in sitting around overanalyzing things for hours like, uh, some people we know. But as I've been told by more than a few girls, our brief, vague responses can often be extremely confusing to you. Below are some prime examples, with my easy translations:

"I'LL CALL YOU" means I haven't decided yet if we should go out or not. That, or I don't like talking on the phone as much as you seem to and dread picking up the receiver because I'm scared I won't have anything to say. I probably will call you, but please don't pin me down on a time, and don't freak out if I call you on a Tuesday when I said I'd call Monday!

"NO, REALLY, THAT'S COOL" usually means the opposite—it isn't (but check the context!). It's a way of being, well, cool—a classic guy maneuver. It also can be a signal to switch the topic, and this comes into play when a subject like a breakup with a former girlfriend is involved. Like when you say, "I hope you don't mind my dating your brother now," and the guy answers, "No, really, that's cool."

**"THAT LOOKS GOOD ON YOU"** means exactly that. A lot of girls think that when we say this, we're lying or we're only saying it because everything else you own makes you look like a troll. Not true. All we mean is that.looks.good.on.you. Period!

**"I'M SORRY"** Too many guys have a hard time saying this, but you already knew that. So when we do apologize, it's a big deal. If a guy says this to you, he almost definitely means it. (Unless he's saying it ten times a day after doing tons of heinous things to you, which means you should already be out the door, anyway.) Take it seriously, and please don't push it with the whole, "But why are you sorry? What are you sorry for?" routine. He knows he hurt you, he feels bad, and he's genuinely trying. Appreciate it. Please?

# CHAPTER TWO:
# WHAT WE LIKE ABOUT YOU

We know that everyone's always telling you how to act, what to wear, what to do in order to get us interested. You're probably pretty confused by now from all the mixed messages. Well, here it is, finally—the real scoop from us . . . about everything we love (and the stuff we don't totally love) about you!

## Positives Attract

Pure, natural enthusiasm is magnetic. I'm not talking about the kind of rah-rah energy that comes with being captain of a cheerleading squad (although if you happen to hold that position, that's great, too!). Even an extra-wide, warm smile and an upbeat attitude can make all the difference.

When I asked 15-year-old Craig why his last relationship didn't work, he didn't even hesitate. "Becky didn't know how to have fun!" he blurted out. "She was such a downer." Apparently she was always complaining about something. Movies were never interesting enough, parties were too boring—life itself was utterly pointless.

"It's not that I expected Becky to like everything," Craig explained once he'd cooled off from his initial burst of anger. "But she never liked anything. My friends and I know how to have a good time even when we're watching really bad movies. We just make fun of all the lame lines or fake-looking special effects. But I don't think I ever saw Becky smile."

As Craig points out, being positive doesn't mean being constantly, perpetually happy. Sometimes life does stink. And if you're going through an especially rough time in your life, then we get why you're going to be bummed out. But if you're never able to crack a smile or find something good from your experiences, chances are you won't be surrounded by boyfriends, either. No one wants to be dragged down like that. So make an effort to find at least a couple of things to make you grin—for your own sake, not ours. After all, whether or not you have a boyfriend doesn't matter if you're not happy with who you are or you can't enjoy anything you do.

### Fight Back

That's right. We like girls who can take us on. Yes, we are competitive, and we do want to win, even against you. Whether it's a card game or a friendly, flirtatious round of "horse" on our driveway basketball net . . . we want to beat you. But that doesn't mean you should let us!

Yeah, maybe we'll be bummed out when you kick our butts. But we'll love you for it in the end. We'll get over the temporary wound to our pride, and we'll be psyched that we have such a cool, talented girlfriend. Just remember—no need to rub your triumph in our faces. Winning? Fine. Gloating? Not fine.

Actually, one of the main things that attracted me to my girlfriend was her competitiveness and her athletic ability. She's a great dancer, with much better rhythm than me (another reason to write this anonymously: I could never admit that to her). That rhythm also translates to the tennis court, where she totally wipes me out. And believe it or not, watching her sweat and bounce around the court to hit killer forehands . . . it's a total turn-on.

Travis, 16, told me he feels the same way about the girl he's had a crush on for two years now. (He refuses to mention her name because he says he's still "working it.") He has known this girl, whom we will call "Amy," since third grade. But it wasn't until she challenged him to a game of one-on-one basketball that Travis started seeing her as more than a friend. He won the game, barely, but that wasn't the point. Amy got really into the game, called fouls and double dribbles, and stole the ball right out of his hands several times. Travis has been head over heels ever since.

Of course, that's not to say you have to annihilate us in every sport or activity known to civilization. I mean, everyone likes to have something they're good at. Just don't hold yourself back—if you've got it in you to win, go for it.

## MELLOW YELLOW

Leave it to us guys to totally contradict ourselves. One second we tell you to be fiercely competitive. The next second we tell you to mellow out. Sorry.

The fact is, as cool as we try to act—in the hallways, around our guy friends, in our cars—we're not as chill as we seem. One of the main reasons why we want so hard to act cool is . . . we're worried that we're not! We're paranoid that we look stupid in these superbaggy jeans, convinced that we just failed our geometry test, and freaking out over whether you think one of our friends is much cuter than we are. Yes, it's true. Underneath the calm surface our minds are going a mile a minute. Major insecurity.

But you can help.

When we say stupid things, try to forgive us. If we're stressed out about something—a big game or our nagging parents—go out of your way to reassure us that it will be okay. Show us you're on our team. Understand that what we really need to take us down from that high-strung obsession with looking "cool" is not for you to get mad and yell at us but to tell us we're gonna do fine in that big game, then hit us on the shoulders. If you really want to chill us out, you could massage those shoulders while you're at it. . . .

## To Each His (and Her!) Own

This may surprise some of you, but we actually don't expect (or even want) you to have identical opinions, thoughts, and tastes to us. Plenty of happy couples have differences, and breakups are rarely caused because of a fight over what to listen to in the car.

I promise—you really don't have to agree with us about every single thing in the universe. Take a stand. If we like vanilla and you think vanilla's boring, put in your vote for double-chocolate fudge mint. We like girls who think for themselves. We even want you to stick up for yourselves if our loser friends say something obnoxious around you. You don't have to stand there and take it!

Of course, there's no reason to go overboard. Having your own ideas is great—trying to push them on us isn't. Just like you have the right to think whatever you want about techno music, Chinese food, and action movies, so do we!

## Eat Up

Rice cakes. Salads. Diet soda. Lean meat on low-fat bread with reduced-calorie dressing. Celery.

Come on.

We want you to eat! We love it when you order the bacon cheeseburger with fries and a Coke and then clean your plate completely. We love wiping a spot of mustard off your chin. We love seeing that you're enjoying food as much as we do!

Yeah, yeah, I know what's coming next. I've heard it from tons of my girl friends before. "You say you like girls who eat, but you want to date skinny girls!" Well, it's not true! We love girls with healthy bodies—hips, curves, the whole deal. And we're turned off by someone who diets and starves herself into a tiny body. I swear.

Besides that, attraction is all about confidence. When you walk around looking like you're happy to be who you are, we're drawn right to you, no matter what your waist size is. And a girl who feels comfortable munching away on a hearty meal looks a lot more appealing to us than the one starving herself in the corner, nibbling away at her carrot. I'm not saying it's wrong to eat healthy stuff—as long as you're doing it for the right reasons. Because cutting out food is not the way to catch our eye.

## GREAT ADVENTURE

Han Solo has Princess Leia. Superman has Lois Lane. Will Smith has Jada Pinkett. We like to consider ourselves rugged, manly adventurers. And we'd love it if our girlfriends would come along for the ride.

Guys are on a constant mission to avoid boredom. If you know how to pull us out of couch–potato mode and plan an activity for us, we'll have major respect for you. The bigger variety of things you're willing to try, the better.

Perfect example: The character played by Cameron Diaz in the movie *There's Something About Mary*. Everyone falls for her because she does so much stuff. She refines her golf swing, plays football, and takes some hacks in a batting cage. But she is also sweet, pretty, and full of energy. We're talking perfect girlfriend material.

Again, this doesn't mean you should pretend to enjoy something you hate. It's just a good idea to be open to new experiences and to have some of your own ideas, too.

Javier, 16, claims that he broke up with his last girlfriend, Jill, because they "never did anything." After two months of dating, Javier got sick of just talking at school, talking on the phone, and watching rented videos together. Jill wasn't interested when Javier suggested they play minigolf, go bowling, or go on a hike. And she never came up with any alternatives herself.

Brendan, 15, couldn't stop glowing to me about his girlfriend, Crystal. Apparently she's even more adventurous than he is. She likes snowboarding and in-line skating and has even gone skydiving! "I think she might be cooler than I am," Brendan said. "But don't tell her I said that."

Sorry, Brendan.

## MYSTERIOUS WAYS

Ok, so now you know we dig a girl who can get active. Don't take this the wrong way or anything, but I'm gonna tell you that we're also into girls who act like (drumroll) . . . girls!

Before you start yelling at me to crawl back into my cave and then slam this book shut, let me say that I know being athletic and adventurous is just as much a part of being a girl as putting on perfume or wearing a skirt. But let's face it—there are still certain basic differences between us. We don't look nearly as good in those skirts as you do! And the thing is, we like to feel like guys. We are genetically programmed to beat our chests and defend you against all evildoers. If we can't actually protect you, we want to feel like we can. And when you break into giggles or smile at us in that feminine, flirtatious way that drives us crazy, we're putty.

Still, if you're a card-carrying tomboy, freak not. I'm not saying you have to wear frills and giggle all the time. My friend Tony's girlfriend, Liza, loves hockey and Sega games almost as much as he does—maybe more. But whenever she flashes him her sweet, killer smile, he melts.

All I'm saying is that we like that you are different from us. We may not understand why certain things— like phones, gossip, and shopping—get many of you excited. That's okay. We can't understand each other all the time—and it's not always such a bad thing. As long as you're comfortable with who you are, we'll be psyched to be around you and to get to know you better.

## MAKE US LAUGH

When they say that the way to a guy's heart is through his stomach, I don't think they're really talking about food. I think they mean the way your stomach hurts after a bout of hysterical, can't-catch-your-breath laughter. Because every guy I talked to named the ability to make him laugh as one of the top features that attracts him to a girl. And yep—I'm included in that category.

That doesn't mean you should all go out and become stand-up comedians. Being funny doesn't have to mean cracking jokes about guys walking into bars with talking parrots on their shoulders. It's just about having a sense of humor—being able to see things that are funny around you and sharing that with us.

Jeff, 14, tends to be a pretty serious guy. When we talked, he barely smiled. So he especially likes it when a girl he's with can make him crack up. He told me that his ex-girlfriend Kim would just give him A Look whenever something hilarious happened—even something that no one but the two of them thought was funny—

and they'd both collapse in giggles. He admitted, in a very wistful tone, it's that Look that he misses most about Kim.

## COMPLIMENTS

You know those huge egos we're supposed to have? The ones you rag on us for all the time? Guess what—it's all a lie. The truth? Our egos are fragile. Very fragile. We all want to think that we're "the maaaaan," whether we are or not. So here's another way to get yourself a permanent place in our hearts—if you think we're all that, make us feel like we are.

There's a science to this. You can't just randomly tell us how great we are. You have to pick something specific, probably something we're proud of or insecure about. Tell us we look cute today, and watch us blush. Tell us you watched our basketball game, and we played really well. If you doubt the importance of this, think about how great you feel when we throw some compliments your way. See, it's easy for you to tell a guy that you're worried about something or need to hear that you look okay/did okay in the play, etc. So we make sure to give your confidence all the boosting we can. (Note—if your guy doesn't do this, then find someone who deserves you and will treat you right!) But we're not supposed to admit that we have less than perfect self-esteem. Some girls don't realize that we need props the same as you. (Please do compliment us! It would make all the difference.)

If you're still skeptical, check out the real-life story of Kyle, 17. During his junior year Kyle developed a crush on his good friend, Jody. Kyle sensed that it wasn't a totally one-way thing, but he wanted to wait for a definite sign before he asked her out. See, Jody was a chronic flirt, and Kyle couldn't tell if her behavior with him was any different from the way she was with her other guy friends or not. Finally, just as Kyle was about to check himself into an insane asylum from trying to figure Jody out, she dropped a huge compliment on him that turned the tides. In a more serious, not as flirty voice she told him what a great dresser he was and how good he looked in his clothes. Kyle asked her out right there, and she said yes. He told me that he has no idea how long it would have taken for him to do that if she hadn't given him that compliment.

I rest my case.

## TEACH AND LEARN

Guys like smart girls. We're not saying you have to be rewiring computers in your spare time or developing the cure for cancer in your private laboratory. Just show us that you know how to think for yourself. That you're

# FIVE WAYS TO START A CONVERSATION WITH A GUY YOU NEVER WANT TO DATE

1. "So, then my ex-boyfriend . . ."

2. "If you just walked a little faster and wore your shirt a little differently. Here, let me show you what you need to change. . . ."

3. "Yeah, I have my period right now, so I have terrible cramps. Actually, I think I'd better go change my tampon. I'll be right back!"

4. "Are you sure that coat's warm enough for this weather? Did you eat enough at lunch today?" (Thanks, Mom!)

5. "You are such a nice guy!"

# Five Ways to Start a Conversation with a Guy You Do Want to Date

1. "Wait—you loved [insert quirky book, movie, or TV show here], too? That was my favorite!"

2. "So, I was thinking about what you were saying yesterday. . . ."

3. "Did you see the Knicks game last night? They really have to start getting more offensive rebounds, but their three-point shooting was awesome."

4. "Yeah, I like hiking and riding my bike—but I'm also fine with just hanging out and watching TV. I'm flexible!"

5. "Did anyone ever tell you that you have really nice eyes?"

interested in knowing more about the world around you. Cheesy, I know, but it makes you seem pretty cool to us.

Ryan, 16, said that he always gets crushes on girls in his English classes. English is his favorite subject, but since he's kind of shy, Ryan rarely speaks in class. But he does listen. At the beginning of every school year Ryan keeps his ears open as the girls in the class talk. One girl, Carrie, has been in Ryan's class for two years in a row. He first started liking her when she analyzed the meaning of Walt Whitman's "Song of Myself." The attraction grew after her on-target reading of *Death of a Salesman*. By the time she was picking apart *Romeo and Juliet*, he had fallen. Hard core.

It's not just about knowing a lot, though. We like it when you share what you know with us—we like to be your "students." Teach us about your world (no preaching though, please), and let us teach you about ours! Deep down we all like to think we're experts at something, and getting the chance to show you our stuff is so cool.

I'm a hockey player, so when my girlfriend asked me to teach her how to in-line skate backward on our fourth date, I was psyched. We went to the park together and began an intensive training session. After a couple of spills she started to wiggle back and forth slowly and finally to skate backward! It was the best feeling for both of us. I could teach. She could skate backward. We could work together. And she looked so cute in skates, shorts, and a grungy T-shirt.

## What's Your Sign?

John was an Aquarius, and he was so sweet. Scorpio boys are wild but fun. You never get along with Capricorns. Actually, that's not true. It's just that Conner was a Capricorn, and he was just so serious and so . . . Capricorn.

Do us a favor, please. Try not to judge us by what month we were born. I have actually managed to scare girls away just by mentioning that I'm a . . . (can you guess it?) Capricorn. One girl whom I'd just met had the nerve to walk away from me, saying, "I can't handle any more Capricorns."

I know there are some guys who get really into astrology, too, but mostly it seems to be a girl thing. It's fine if you want to read your horoscope—or ours. But please don't act like who we are is completely determined by whether we're a Taurus or a Pisces. Give us a chance. . . .

## Call the Shots

Take the initiative. Go on, take it! Ask us out. Plan the date for us. Tell us what you thought of the movie before we even open our mouths.

Brad, 17, says his ex-girlfriends always expected him to lead the way. On Friday nights he would be the one finding out where the fun party was or choosing what channel they would watch on TV. Even during late-night instant messages, Brad would have to decide what they would chat about.

All that changed when he met Meredith. "She always has suggestions about where we can go, things we can do for fun," Brad told me with this goofy, amazed grin. "Being with her is such a breeze." Meredith is an outdoorsy type—hiking is her favorite hobby. After she had brought Brad along a couple of times when they first started seeing each other, he got really into it. He even went out and bought himself real hiking boots. Brad's gotten Meredith into some of his hobbies, too—like watching foreign films. Brad claims that Meredith is the first girl he's dated who wasn't afraid to take over sometimes, and instead of getting lazy because of it, he's even more inspired to come up with his own ideas, too.

It's not that we want you to control us or tell us what to do every second of the day. Not at all. But we like it when you're independent enough to make decisions and stick with them.

## One of the Guys

Sometimes it seems like we're locked forever in one of those school dances where girls sit on one side of the room and guys sit on the other. You know how those go—everybody stares across the room at one anther, anxiously wondering who's going to make the first move.

Why can't we just chill out a little and cross that divide? It doesn't even have to be about love connections. We need to be friends, too. Sure, there are times when we just want to hang with our guys. Play a few video games, watch some ESPN, or talk about you. But having girls around can make life a lot more interesting and fun, and we definitely want more of it.

I know a lot of you worry that if you become our "buddy," we won't look at you as girlfriend material anymore. I'm not going to lie—this does happen. And it goes both ways. I had a huge crush on my friend Kim for years, and it killed me when she told me that she "just couldn't see me that way" because since I hung out a lot with her and a few other girls, I was practically one of their group. Not a guy-guy. Ouch.

But despite this danger, it's still worth the risk. Overall, if you show us that you can be comfortable hanging around us as a friend, we'll respect you more. We'll get to know you better, and you'll get to know us better. (You might even learn something I missed!) What could be wrong with that?

## Facing the Music

We all have different tastes in music. I can't stand the stuff my friend Rick puts on when he gets in my car, and he hates every CD I own. But we're still as close as brothers. It's the same for guys and girls—you don't have to love our music to love us.

Steven, 16, is a music fanatic. He described to me the way the walls of his bedroom are totally obscured by the thousands of CDs stacked high in numerous cases. That doesn't mean any girl he dates has to like—or even know—every group he listens to. But she should understand what music means to him, the same way you'd want your boyfriend to care about something that's important to you.

Music's a pretty big deal to a lot of guys—and a lot of girls, too. We can probably be bigger snobs about it, though—sometimes. My brother's nose automatically raises a few centimeters in the air when the name "Backstreet Boys" comes up in conversation. But if you're a fan of BSB, Britney Spears, or any other musician we don't happen to love, you don't have to hide it. What kind of a jerk wouldn't make up his mind about you based on who you are instead of what you listen to? I mean, would you hold it against a guy if he wasn't groovin' to the reggae tunes you adore or an equally big fan of whatever kind of music you listen to? And you know what else? I've heard my brother hum along to BSB's "Quit Playing Games (with My Heart)" when he thinks no one's around.

## Shop Till We Pop

Brace yourself for this revelation—most guys don't like to shop. Surprised? Probably not. The thought of hanging out all day in a store, trying on clothes, just doesn't give us the same excitement it seems to give you. And waiting outside while you try on clothes? Even worse.

Jared, 16, swore to me that he's really patient when his girlfriend, Lindsay, brings him shopping with her. Okay, so maybe he rolls his eyes when—after six solid hours of trying on dresses—she walks away empty-handed. But he still sticks it out with her.

Little lesson? Jared's a major exception. Most of us would go crazy if we had to put up with a day like that. Dave, 16, and his girlfriend, Jenny, also 16, say they have a perfect solution: the mall. While she searches for the black sling-back sandals she's dying for, he's free to cruise through the music stores, grab some snacks in the food court, or even sneak in a couple of quick games in the arcade.

"Guys don't shop to feel good," Dave explains. "We

shop because we need something. That's it." But if you come up with a good diversion tactic, like Dave and Jenny's compromise, it could work.

Why is it so tough for us to endure the shopping rituals you seem to adore so much? Mainly it's because we're very goal oriented. We need to see tangible success achieved, so we feel the mission was a failure if we walk out of the store without a full shopping bag. If a guy heads to the Gap for a sweater, he must leave with one, even if it's not his first choice. Otherwise the afternoon was a waste. And if it's you with the empty hands? Somehow it's just as frustrating to know that we've spent all this time helping you on a failed enterprise. The same goes for "window shopping," that bizarre nonactivity that so many of you enjoy. What's the point? And believe me—there needs to be a point if we're going to take part in it.

The best plan is to save those full-day intensive mall trips for your girlfriends and bring us along only when there's a clear-cut goal that we can accomplish in less time than it takes to, oh, I don't know—prepare a feast for an army.

## SPINNING THE RUMOR MILL

Rumors happen. It's a fact of life, like scary cafeteria food and bad grades. But you don't have to believe everything you hear—and you don't have to pass it on, either. How about a deal? We won't listen to what people say about you if you make an effort to ignore what they say about us! Otherwise we could end up like these guys:

"THIS ONE GIRL I REALLY LIKED HEARD SOMEWHERE THAT I GET OBSESSED WITH MY GIRLFRIENDS AND THAT I'M CONSTANTLY JEALOUS, SO SHE WOULDN'T GO OUT WITH ME. I WISH I COULD HAVE TOLD HER I WAS ONLY LIKE THAT WITH ONE GIRLFRIEND TWO YEARS AGO AND HAVE GROWN UP A LOT SINCE." —TODD, 16, PROVIDENCE, RI

"MY FIRST YEAR AT SLEEP-AWAY CAMP I CRIED ONCE BECAUSE I WAS HOMESICK. WELL, BY THE TIME THAT STORY MADE THE ROUNDS, THE DETAILS WERE ALL WRONG. IT SOUNDED LIKE I STILL CRIED MYSELF TO SLEEP EVERY NIGHT, AND THIS GIRL BLEW ME OFF BECAUSE OF IT. I JUST WISH SHE'D GIVEN ME THE CHANCE TO DEFEND MYSELF." —RYAN, 17, DAYTONA BEACH, FL

"ONE TIME THESE GIRLS I KNEW SPREAD THIS RUMOR THAT MY LAST GIRLFRIEND DUMPED ME BECAUSE I HAD BAD BREATH. WELL, I FINALLY

ASKED THE EX, AND SHE DENIED SAYING IT. BUT NOW THE GIRLS I MEET ARE SCARED TO KISS ME!" —ROB, 14, COLUMBUS, OH

## OFF-LIMITS

It seems like keeping journals is a big deal to you—at least many of you. Sure, some of us have tried to write in them, too, but they usually end up just like the rest of our big plans and dead-end hobbies.

Here's the problem: We know it's wrong to snoop in your journals. We wouldn't like it if we caught you sneaking around our bedrooms. But sometimes it's hard to resist a peek, especially if the book falls into our laps. We can't help thinking that maybe you wrote about us in there. And then that good old insecurity flares up, pushing us to know the truth about how much you really like us.

I nicknamed my old girlfriend Tara the "Mad Scribbler." Whenever we got into a fight, she would immediately turn to her journal. It was automatic; if she got mad, she would start scribbling. It drove me completely nuts until one day when I did something about it.

We were driving to this class picnic when Tara and I got into a stupid fight about why I had an ex-girlfriend's mix tape in my car. I told Tara the tape had great songs on it, and I never even really thought about who had made it for me. That somehow made her angrier. She accused me of not caring about the mixes she had made for me and asked me why I wasn't listening to them.

Anyway, after this battle she pulled her light blue journal out of her backpack and started scribbling. I tried to focus on my driving, but I couldn't help looking over every couple of minutes. She had her typical scrunched-up expression, focused and furious. I kept quiet.

Well, we went to the picnic and pretty much forgot the whole tape fight ever happened. Until later. When I got back to the car, Tara's journal was beneath the passenger seat. It must have slipped out of her backpack when she climbed out of the car. Tara had left with a few of her friends, so I was alone. Alone with her private, for-her-eyes-only journal. The one that could possibly contain vast insight into what Tara actually thought about me.

I knew it was wrong, but I sat down and opened the book, flipping right to the last page. I was surprised to find out that the stuff she'd written today wasn't even about our fight. It was just all these interesting thoughts, about herself and how she reacted to things. It just made me feel like scum for reading it. Tara had all these cool things to say, but they were her personal words, and I'd read them without her permission.

I never told Tara what I did. What was the point? I knew she would just get angry. But I swore I would never do it again.

It's tough for us to resist the temptation to peek inside. If you're looking for a way to ward us off, try talking to us about what purpose your journal serves. In other words, make it crystal clear that it's not just a book to express the evil that is us. (Did I mention we're a little self-centered and tend to think everyone's worlds revolve around us?) Explain to your boyfriend that it's just a place to vent, to process your thoughts, or to express yourself. It's still hard for us not to pry, but if you explain that there may not be as much juicy stuff in there as we think, that will help.

And finally, on a more practical note, don't tempt us. Try not to leave your journal out when you're not around, and maybe keep that e-mail password a secret.

## THE TRAPS: WHAT GIRLS MEAN WHEN THEY SAY . . .

We're confused by a lot of what you say, a lot of the time. But we've learned to fear certain statements more than others, to cringe automatically when one slips out of your mouth. Here's why we get so nervous:

**"DO I LOOK FAT?"** The obvious answer to this question is no, right? Well, I've tried that one. And what do I get in return? I'm lying. I'm not even paying attention. Or I don't care enough to notice that she's gained three point two pounds in the past week and her jeans are fitting slightly more snugly. Why do you still ask this? If you're convinced that the answer is yes (when it probably isn't, anyway), then nothing we say is going to change your mind. Can't you just realize that we wouldn't be with you if we didn't think you were an amazing, wonderful, gorgeous creature?

**"I DON'T WANT TO TALK ABOUT IT."** Actually, you do. Right? This seems to be what you say when we've gotten to the core of something that's really bothering you. We hear, "I don't want to talk about it with you." We know that your gender is into the whole sharing-your-feelings thing, so why are you suddenly clamming up with us? Did we do something horribly wrong? Do you just (gulp) not like us anymore? Please clarify this statement, especially when it comes out right after you've been on the phone with your best friend for hours!

**"NO, I'M NOT MAD."** Well, you certainly look it. Your face is red. Your arms are crossed. No eye contact. When the Mad Scribbler used to tell me this, I would keep pestering her until she got so annoyed that she would admit that yes, she was mad. Especially after I'd just been bothering her about it for the past five minutes! But I didn't know what else to do to get her to be honest. Do us a favor and tell the truth. Let us know when you're angry and tell us why, too. There's nothing more frustrating than the old, "If you don't know why, then I'm not going to tell you," line. I swear—we really don't know why! But if you explain it, there's a great chance it will never happen again. Doesn't that make it worth your while?

**"I THINK WE SHOULD JUST BE FRIENDS."** Oh, the agony. This one's pretty easy to get, right? We know you're actually saying that you feel zero attraction to us, which does quite a number on our pride. And we never believe you mean that you still want to talk to us, hang out—you know, be friends. All we heard is that you're not dying to throw yourself at our studly bodies, and we're too crushed to get beyond that. So here's a tip: Let a little time go by for us to nurse our bruised egos, then give us a call to show that you're serious about the whole friendship thing.

# CHAPTER THREE:
# LOOKING
# GOOD

"It's what's on the inside that counts."

How many times have you heard that? Well, it's basically true. What's most important is all that stuff we told you about in the last chapter—being positive, funny, smart, adventurous, and knowing how to act around us.

But if you want total honesty, then I have to admit that doesn't mean we're not checking you out. We are. But is that so bad? You put effort into looking good, right? And all we're doing is appreciating it. Read on to discover our true opinions on your appearances—from head to toe.

## You, You, You!

Your clothes should be a reflection of you—of your individual style. If all of your friends are wearing capri pants because they're the new "thing" right now but you think they're stupid, don't wear them. All you'll do is blend in more with the crowd, making it tougher for us to spot your stunning self!

In school my friends and I had these dorky little code names for the girls we liked. I called Beth "V neck" because almost every one of her shirts had that same V-necked cut. It was something small, but it was still distinctive from everyone else. So whether you end up being some guy's "bracelet girl" for the jangly silver bracelets you always wear or another guy's "sweater girl" because of your collection of soft, fuzzy sweaters, remember to dress in a way that fits your identity. Go to thrift shops or Abercrombie & Fitch, whatever you like, as long as you make sure you look like you.

## Stylin'

Here I go again with the hypocrite problem. I've just told you to find your own specific, different look, and now I'm about to lump a bunch of styles into stereotyped categories. Unfair, I know. But you've got to admit—there are certain types of clothes. And it's not hard to make the leap from there to figuring out some basic things about the girl wearing that particular outfit. Not the most sophisticated system, but you're dealing with people who will often give a "smell test" to the clothes on our floor to see if they're wearable. Anyway, here's what the guys I talked to have to say about these common "types":

**"PREPPY PERFECT"** Think Reese Witherspoon in *Election*. This girl uses a headband so not one hair falls out of place. She also prefers skirts, conservative sweaters, and plaid patterns. Most guys agree that this look inspires respect but can also be very intimidating. "I'm afraid she's staring at the stain on my shirt or wondering why my pants are wrinkled," Josh, 15, says. It takes a pretty confident guy to approach a girl with this style. If you fit into this group, be aware of that and try to give an extra-warm smile to a guy you're interested in so that he knows there's much more to you than your perfectly pressed clothes.

**"THRIFT STORE QUEEN"** One day she might wear a beat-up denim jacket she got for two bucks at the Salvation Army. The next she wears purple sunglasses she scored for a nickel at a tag sale. Guys say they tend to admire her originality and assume that she'll be interesting to hang out with. Josh, however, pointed out that "sometimes a girl like this can be sort of snobby. Like judging me because I forgot to recycle my can at lunch or something." Note to all thrift store queens: Make it clear that you're not the recycling police. Just because you wear funky-looking clothes doesn't mean you're going to hold our Gap khakis against us, right?

**"GOTHIC GIRL"** This girl is big on the color black. She might have a bunch of piercings or other kinds of body art, too. We totally respect the individuality and wild, adventurous spirit that this look suggests. But Josh again (he got pretty talkative on the subject of clothes!) pointed out the potential problem here. This style can definitely send out a message that you're a major gloom-and-doom girl. Maybe you just like to dress this way but you're actually open to a good time. If so, it's really important that you flash that same smile I advised the "preppy perfect" types to give, just to show you're not all about darkness.

**"GIRL NEXT DOOR"** Sigh. My personal favorite, I admit. This look is inspired by shows like *Felicity* or *Dawson's Creek*, and it usually involves a lot of khaki and solid-colored shirts. Gap and J. Crew make their living off of these girls. The big word here is comfort. Not just the fit of the clothes, but the feeling we get around you. We're comfortable around girls who dress this way, and there isn't much of an intimidation risk like with some of the other styles. However, you do want to avoid the "dull" trap that comes with looking like every other girl who shops in these stores. Add a touch of your own personality to the outfit, like funky socks or a cool necklace, and you'll set yourself apart.

## Up, Down, and All Around

We might not notice every single time you get a haircut, but we definitely spend a lot of time staring at your hair. It's another part of what makes you different from us— short or long, straight or curly, it's girl hair. We can't wait for the chance to run our fingers through it!

When it comes down to it, there really isn't any one "type" of hair that all guys prefer. Yeah, some guys dig shoulder-length reddish brown waves, and others have a soft spot for long black curls. But we're open to all kinds of styles and colors. Just don't overdo it on products. Like I said, we want to be able to touch your hair, so it shouldn't seem stiff and frozen from a combination of sprays, gels, and mousses.

So don't waste all that time figuring out how to style your hair so we'll fall for you. Wear it however it feels right to you, and we'll probably dig it, too!

## Making It Up

I know guys are always saying, "You don't need to wear any makeup!" And, "I like the natural look!" And then you snicker because the "natural look" your boyfriend just complimented you on was achieved after fifteen minutes in front of the mirror. But the truth is, we've probably seen you without makeup, and you really don't need it. Still, a lot of you like to wear it, we know. And that's okay. Really. But I wouldn't be honest if I didn't mention a few quick pointers on our biggest likes and dislikes:

- Avoid overdoing those ultrabright colors, like pale blue eye stuff that goes all the way up to your eyebrows, or hot pink circles on your cheeks.

- Just like we go for hair that looks touchable, we love lips that seem kissable. So those shimmery, glossy lipsticks are great. They give your lips a nice shine, making them look like . . . well, the way they do when we kiss you! And being reminded of that experience is never a bad thing.

- Again, if it were up to us, you wouldn't need to put

anything on your eyes. But if you're going to, at least try to avoid heavy, clumpy dark eyeliner circling your eyes—the raccoon effect is not good.

## BODY TALK

Contrary to what every one of you seems to think, we aren't looking for Barbie dolls. We're attracted to all kinds of different body types as long as they look natural and healthy. And yeah, some guys have their preferences. You probably do, too, right? That whole "tall, dark, and handsome" bit didn't come from nowhere. But for every guy who adores short girls, there's one who lives for tall girls. And if you happen to be on the shorter side and you meet a tall-girl fan but end up connecting, I promise you that he will not hold the height issue against you. Haven't you ever fallen for someone who doesn't fit your exact type?

This goes for the rest, too. Yes, we like breasts. (Of course we do—it's something else that we don't have!) We like legs. We like butts. But we like them in all different varieties. I swear. There have been entire songs written about different guys' preferences for bigger or smaller breasts, butts, and all other body parts. One more thing—I know you get annoyed when you catch us staring if you're wearing something a little tight or revealing. Now, your wearing that stuff gives us no right to touch you without your consent or in any way harass you. But if we steal a tiny glimpse now and then, can you forgive us?

Let me repeat one more time, for those of you who will have trouble believing me—we do not want you to make yourselves skinny for us. A girl who actually eats is a lot more fun to be around because she isn't totally obsessed with starving herself. That doesn't mean that if you happen to have been born with a thin body type, we won't be into it. We just don't want you to force yourself to look like someone you're not.

Benji, 17, has a pretty serious story on this subject. When he started dating Robyn, he thought she was great looking. But after a couple of months of eating in the school cafeteria with her, he realized that something was wrong. She only ordered salads, and then she didn't even finish them. Even worse, she talked about food all the time, going on and on about what sounded good and what looked good on his plate. The bonier Robyn got, the harder it was for Benji to feel attracted to her. He could tell she wasn't healthy. After months of coaxing her, Benji finally helped Robyn to see that she needed medical help. Luckily she was able to get better, with Benji's support.

Benji is one of the good ones. There might be some jerks out there who will pressure you to change your appearance for them—lose weight, gain weight, dye your hair, whatever. But these guys are just that: jerks. They aren't worth a millisecond of your time, and if the guy you're dating starts acting like that, get rid of him. Fast.

You are born with a certain body type. You can take care of your body by eating well and getting enough exercise, but there are things you'll never be able to change. And that's a good thing! Guys have so many different tastes—and we don't want you all to look the same. Trust me.

### HEAVEN SCENT

Brett, 15, said that the smell of his girlfriend's perfume was what first drew him to her. "She walked past me the first day of biology, and I felt my heart start pounding like crazy," Brett told me, shaking his head. "She smelled so good, like honey. I could barely take it."

As weird as it sounds, a lot of food-derived scents are popular. Many guys will go for perfumes with hints of cinnamon or vanilla. It's cool if you have a distinctive smell—a certain fragrance that will always remind us of you. If you're not into perfume, it can even be something you use in your hair. My ex used this great apple-scented conditioner. It made me want to stay close to her all the time!

The overall point to keep in mind here is (once again) not to overdo it. Josh, our fashion expert, says he "can't stand" when a girl wears one of those really heavy perfumes, the ones where you can still smell it in the air even when she walked away five minutes ago. So just dab on something light, sweet, and fresh—and if you like it, chances are we will, too!

## PIERCE THIS

Guys are pretty much all over the place when it comes to piercings. Some of us love it; others hate it. Many more don't care either way. A few guys might even be a little intimidated.

Mike, 16, has three hoops in one ear and one through his eyebrow. Because being pierced is really important to him, he likes to date girls who have piercings, too. Enter Suzie, with a silver stud right through her tongue that flashes every time she talks. Mike thinks it's one of the coolest things he's ever seen.

But Mike's friend Sean disagrees. "It's not that I don't like piercings," Sean explains. "I do. But only on someone like Gwen Stefani." Sean admits that a nose ring or belly-button ring is pretty much the most he could deal with.

The lesson here shouldn't be too surprising. Do your own thing—whatever works for you—and you'll find a

# Five
# Instant Turn-offs

1. Huge, overstyled hair—the kind that can make you a whole foot taller

2. Spending too much time fussing with your hair or makeup or staring into every mirror you pass

3. Trying too hard for a "look" that obviously doesn't fit your personality

4. Fake, orange-looking tan

5. Obvious bad attitude—like a big pout

guy who is looking for exactly your type, whether you have piercings all over or never even got your ears pierced!

## Eye to Eye

One time after hockey practice I asked a locker room full of guys what part of a girl's body they liked best. You can probably guess some of the parts I expected to hear, especially considering the macho factor of the locker room. But I was surprised to hear a variety of interesting answers. One guy liked shoulders; two guys were into hands; some said faces. The most popular answer? Eyes.

I had never really noticed eyes that much, but from that day on, I started looking into girls' eyes when I talked to them. And now I understand what those guys in the locker room meant.

Every guy has different taste in eye color, so you shouldn't freak out if you don't have baby blue or piercing green eyes. "I've always been into brown-eyed girls," says Kobe, 18.

The best part of eyes, no matter what the shape, size, or color, is how you use them to express your feelings. It's pretty hard to resist it when you flash us one of those warm, soft, intense looks. And there's no better way to let a guy know you're interested than the old eye-

# GIRLS WHO WEAR GLASSES

When I met my friend Teri, she wore contact lenses. Every day in homeroom Teri's eyes would be tearing up, and she would have to pour all these solutions into her eyes just to keep them open and red-free. It looked painful. She finally admitted to me that she did own a pair of glasses but refused to wear them because supposedly they looked "hideous" on her.

After a couple of weeks of my watching her strain to deal with the lenses when they obviously irritated her pretty hazel eyes, I begged her to try on the glasses.

It turned out her glasses were these supercool plastic frames. They looked great on her, and after I convinced her to wear them to school, she got compliments all day long. Her eyes were a lot more comfortable without any watery contacts stuck in them, and she looked incredible.

So don't believe that old line about guys not liking girls who wear glasses. If you find a funky pair like Teri had, we'll probably love it. And we'd definitely prefer it to you stumbling around blindly or forcing yourself to wear contacts if they bother you.

lock trick. Kobe says that what attracted him to his current girlfriend, Kendra, was the way she'd make eye contact when they passed each other in the hallway. The way she fixed her gaze on his with just the right amount of intensity and interest drove him crazy. He had to ask her out.

So remember—your eyes are one of your best assets!

# CHAPTER FOUR

# DATING, LOVE, & EVERYTHING IN BETWEEN

We've seen you looking at us, and we've been looking right back. Our friends have started to talk. How do we get from here . . . to there? How do we let you know we like you without making fools of ourselves? And what about first dates? Where do we take you? How do we act? What happens if we hook up? What about if we break up? Believe it or not, these and many more questions all whirl through our minds at a frightening pace. You heard it here—guys are just as scared about dating, relationships, and falling in love as you are.

## THE DATING GAME

You would think that by now we would have figured out a perfect formula for how to ask you out. I mean, we helped put people on the moon and cheese into a can, but we still haven't hit on a solution for this? It's sad. And what's even sadder is that we're so afraid of rejection, many of us never even reach the "how to ask you out," stage. We're still stuck at level one—wondering if we can.

There are some guys out there with serious confidence. Guys who can walk right up to a girl and just say something as simple as, "Do you want to go out sometime?" Sigh. Yeah, there are guys like that. But the majority of us only wish we could be so bold. So if a guy does come up to you and asks you out on the spot, be impressed. Be flattered. It is not easy.

One of the more popular approaches from those of us who are, ahem, not so endowed in the courage department is to call you on the phone. While this is a common strategy, this tactic has its problems, too. Although we don't have to be intimidated by the sight of cute, appealing you in person, we do have to use a device with which we are not particularly skilled. Calling a girl out of the blue and making small talk can be downright terrifying.

Doug, 16, says he used to have a terrible time getting a first date over the phone because he would panic and babble all kinds of random, silly stuff. One time he totally messed things up by talking about the last girl who dumped him!

"I felt like such a loser," Doug confessed, sinking a little lower in his chair. "I finally decided it was better just to let the girl do most of the talking." He invented his own rule: Stay on for fifteen minutes, then ask The Question. So far, it's only worked once, but that's one more than his past track record. "It will be my golden rule," Doug promised me, "for now at least."

My friend Joey uses the grapevine strategy. When he first met Stephanie, he went straight to her friends, found out if she was single, then dropped all these hints about how he thought she was so cute and nice. He didn't call her until he was sure all the vibes he was getting back from her friends were positive. If your friends mention that a guy's been digging around for info with them, try not to get mad or offended. He's probably just too shy to come straight to you. As long as he isn't asking anything too personal or being obnoxious about it, give him a chance to prove that he can carry on a conversation with you once that initial scary moment of asking you out is over.

Most guys agree that asking girls out is one of the

scariest things we ever have to do. The worst thing that can happen is when you treat our question as a joke or blow us off without a second thought. Ever done that to a guy? There's a good chance he hasn't asked a single girl out since. A no is okay if you're just not interested. That's definitely better than leading us on. But at least take us seriously, and respect our feelings. Even if we sometimes hide them really well, we do have them.

## SADIE HAWKINS TIME

Since I've just finished explaining how incredibly hard it is for us to ask you out, it shouldn't come as a surprise that I am all for the tables being turned. When you make the first move, it takes a lot of the pressure off of us, which is a huge relief.

My friend Paul didn't have a big problem asking girls out. He was pretty popular, and he'd never been rejected in one of those painful, heart-ripped-out-of-you ways. (Can you guess that I'm a little more familiar with that experience?) Anyway, when school started our senior year, he'd barely had time to fix up his locker when this new girl Nicole walked right up to him and asked if he wanted to go out for ice cream after school.

Nicole was very pretty, but the thing that really blew Paul away was how forward she was. He wasn't used to girls asking him out like that, and he was very impressed.

He said yes, and they dated for about a month.

Of course, as easy as it would be if there was a simple formula, I'm the first to admit that not every guy responds well to being asked out directly.

Robert, another friend of mine, met Leslie through his part-time job at a bookstore. Robert thought she was really cute, and he told me they flirted more than they worked. He'd been trying to work up the courage to ask her out when suddenly one day—wham—Leslie invited him to come with her to a friend's party. Taken off guard and feeling like he'd failed somehow by not being the first one to get the question out, Robert completely bailed.

It took a couple of phone calls to get all the details. But the story was, Robert was convinced that Leslie thought he had dropped the ball by not asking before she did. (I tried to explain that it obviously wasn't the case since she wouldn't have asked him out if she was upset with him, but somehow this logic escaped him.) Now, understandably, you don't want to end up with a guy whose ego black-and-blues that easily, anyway. Shouldn't the chance to go out with fabulous you be more important than hurt pride? Yes, it should. But just so you know, there will be times when he won't see it this way. Try not to take it too personally. If a guy's been giving you all the right signals, then freaks when you ask him out, this is probably why. Give him some time, and maybe he'll come around.

So how do you know when to ask and when not to ask? If I knew a surefire way to tell, I would have patented it long ago and I'd be lying on my own private little island right now. Sorry. But I do know one helpful trick that will work in many situations. If you sense that the guy you like is shy, why not give him as many hints as possible that you're interested, then wait a little longer for him to ask you out?

My friend Jim had been into Liz for a while, but he just hadn't been able to ask her out. Finally at this Halloween party Liz got so fed up with Jim's mixed signals that she sent her friend Jessie to go talk to him. Jessie made sure to give Jim the clear idea that Liz really liked him, finally breaking him out of his fear.

When they were done, Jim walked over to Liz and didn't leave her side all night. They ended up staying together for over a year.

Liz later confessed to Jim that she'd put Jessie up to the conversation that had motivated him to come over. But at the time Jim thought he was making the first move, which made all the difference.

For the most part, we're pretty clueless when it comes to knowing where we stand with you. You might think you're being really obvious, but if we're not

# THE "FIRST SIGHT" PHENOMENON

I've heard a lot of girls say that they can fall in love with a guy at first sight. For us, though, it's not so common. We can see you and think you're pretty or that you have a great laugh or lots of interesting things to say. We can even develop major crushes on you after that first conversation. But love? We're not so quick to jump into it or to use the word. So try not to get hurt if it takes us a little longer. It's just because we want to really mean it when we say it. And that can't be a bad thing, right?

picking up on it—be more obvious.

Then again, if you're sending out a strong vibe for a while without getting any response, it may be time to look elsewhere. Sadly, crushes and love are not always mutual. But remember—although making the move can definitely be scary, rejection really isn't the end of the world.

## NERVES OF COTTON

I've sat in on enough "gossip" sessions with my female friends to know what happens to you when you spot your crush coming down the hall. Your heart flutters. Your stomach lurches. What will I say to him? Why didn't I wear my red skirt today instead of these raggedy old jeans? Is he coming toward me?

By no means do you have an exclusive claim to this oh-my-God-what-do-I-do-now syndrome that accompanies a crush sighting. As I've already told you, guys feel the need to act cool, but inside we're just as freaked out about messing things up with the girls we like. Did you get that? Yes, it's the truth—you make us nervous, too. So when we do get up the guts to go talk to you and all you do is stare at the floor, fiddle with your notebook, or tuck your hair behind your ears a million times, it makes the whole thing that much harder on us. Maybe you're really nervous—or maybe you can't stand us and just wish we'd leave you alone already.

So if a certain guy always makes your heart do backward flips in your chest, try to prepare yourself a little the next time you see him. Take a deep breath, slow down your thoughts, and make yourself meet his eye. We know it's tough, but we managed to make the first move. So can't you do us a favor and tame the jittery thing a bit? Let him speak first if you want. Then ask questions to take the pressure off you. And keep telling yourself: It's no big deal. He's not that cute. All right, maybe he is that cute, but it's still no big deal. . . .

## Where Are Your Manners?

Okay, so we've asked you out, or you've asked us out, or our best friends fixed us up. Somehow we ended up on a date together. Now what are we supposed to do?

We've all grown up hearing about those "rules" of dating. Like, how we're supposed to hold doors, pull out chairs, pay the bill. But then we've also heard girls say it's rude to do those things—it's sexist. All of this information blends together in our brains and leaves us complete nervous wrecks. We're scared that no matter what we do, we'll offend you.

How can you help? Early on in the date, let us know what you're expecting. If his waiting for you to sit down first is too much, then just smile and wave it off. Act like it's no big deal, and the guy will take the hint. Or grab the door and hold it for your date one time so he'll see he doesn't have to always do it.

"I think I used to go totally overboard," Lenny, 17, admitted to me. "I would even insist that the girl sat facing the restaurant." He explained that a lot of this had to do with the way his parents had raised him and how they'd taught him about manners. "But most girls just thought it was weird," he continued. "They said they really didn't care about that stuff." Since then Lenny says he makes an effort to be nice and attentive without making the girl feel awkward. "It makes my dates a lot more relaxing," he added with a smile.

Holding doors is one thing but who pays is another issue entirely. Even if we want to do the "gentlemanly" thing here, we can't always do it. We usually have as much money as you do (which is basically spare change). Remember: We're in school most of the day, too. When you offer to split the bill, we know that you appreciate our limited cash flow. It works out well at the movies, for example, when one person pays for the tickets and the other handles popcorn and sodas. That way it still feels like you're "treating" each other to things.

"If I have some extra cash on me, I don't mind paying," Dave, 16, said. "As long as I'm not expected to pay every time." Dave says he will still offer to pay on the first date, just to be polite, but he hopes the girl will insist on at least chipping in.

On dates we usually take our cues from you, so give us a little help here—show us how you want us to act and try not to make us feel like we've failed if we can't afford to take you on an all-expenses-paid dream date. It will make the night so much more fun!

## Movie Madness

If I asked you to name the most common date activity, you'd probably say, "Going to a movie." That's what most of the guys I interviewed came up with. Movies are great for giving you a shared experience without the pressure of having to talk to each other for a little while. Sitting next to each other in the dark theater is very romantic, and when the movie's over, you've got an instant conversation starter.

So where's the problem here? It comes down to this—different tastes. When the all-important decision of what to see must be made, it's often the cause of serious tension between us.

Chuck, 14, loves sci-fi flicks. Unfortunately, when he started dating Erin, a redhead he'd liked for years, he discovered that she couldn't stand science fiction. Instead of compromising for the first few dates and seeing his choice movies with other friends, Chuck dragged Erin along to three sci-fi movies in a row, convinced that he could convert her. The first movie Erin tolerated. The second one she napped through. By the third time she started to get mad.

"He would be all vague about where we were going," Erin told me. "And then each time we'd end up at the same movie theater, and he'd walk up and buy tickets to a movie he knew I didn't want to see."

Chuck, like many of my fellow guys, was a little slow on the uptake. Erin made the right move by finally putting her foot down and refusing to go see one more movie about hybrid alien races. If she hadn't said anything, he could have easily interpreted her lack of protest as a slowly developing taste for the genre. So speak up! If you don't want to see the kind of movies he's bringing you to, let him know.

If he's not interested in your top picks, either, your best bet might be to find a good compromise movie. Something with enough action, humor, plot, or emotion to keep both of you happy—whatever your personal tastes are.

## It's a Group Thing

There's no denying that group dates can be great icebreakers, especially when you're going out with someone you don't know very well yet—or even with a blind date. In a group context there are plenty of other girls and guys around, so the spotlight's not on the two of you the whole night. There isn't as much danger of those awkward silences because plenty of people are there to fill them.

The flip side here is that there also isn't a chance to get to know each other as well. You can't ask personal questions at the bowling alley with a bunch of your friends around. While this can make the date less stressful, it keeps you from building the closeness that you'll need to become a couple. Another problem is that

# Five Fast and Efficient Relationship Killers

1. Practicing your acceptance speech for prom king and queen as the school's supercouple—after just two dates
2. Using cutesy voices in front of his friends
3. Expecting to be together 24/7—and throwing a fit if you're not
4. Overacting the part of the helpless princess or damsel in distress and expecting him to do/plan/think of everything
5. Flirting with his friends

it's difficult to predict the chemistry of big groups. The guys could go into "macho mode" around their friends, while the girls could huddle together and do that cliquey thing you do sometimes.

Basically, group dates can work very early on if you're both paralyzed by nerves or once you're actually a long-term couple and you already know each other well. But if the first date or two you go on with someone is a group thing, make sure you go out one-on-one next. The solo date has plenty of advantages, anyway, right?

## Hooking Up

First kisses are one of the greatest inventions ever. Okay, so I guess they don't exactly count as an invention, although someone figured out that locking lips was a lot more fun than that little nose-rubbing ritual that came first, right?

Here's the thing: We all love kissing, but unfortunately a kiss can mean a lot of different things. And even more unfortunately, sometimes a kiss means different things to the two people who are sharing it. When you're caught up in the moment, all you want to do is kiss that person. But then the next day you might start to think about it and realize that you two really work better as friends. Or maybe everything's great at first, but in a few weeks you begin to not get along so well.

There are so many possible reasons for a great kiss not to lead to a relationship, like if an ex-girlfriend comes back into the picture, if we don't see you for a long time after the kiss and one or both of us has changed, or if we simply weren't looking for something serious. Yeah, it hurts when you're expecting a hookup to mean more, but please know that it's not always about you.

When it comes down to it, we like to go slowly—at least with emotional stuff. It's pretty tough to resist getting close to you, but then when we have to face all the emotional consequences, a lot of us get scared. Can we really open up to you? Let ourselves get close? Tell you the name of the stuffed animal we slept with when we were kids or admit how afraid we are that our parents are disappointed in us? Relationships mean making ourselves vulnerable, and that's a terrifying thing for guys (girls, too, I know). We protect those inner cores with everything we've got.

Usually—though definitely not always—hooking up with you means that we are interested in taking things further. But it still doesn't mean the relationship is set in stone. "I normally won't kiss a girl unless I know I want to go out with her," Lee, 15, said. "But I have done it before," he admitted.

Apparently last summer Lee was a counselor at a camp, where he became good friends with Linda. On the last night he ended up hooking up with her. "But then we went back to school, and it got really hard to keep in touch," Lee explained. Long-distance romance is a possibility, but it's really tough to make it work—especially for a relationship that's just starting out.

Sometimes the best way to know what you're getting into is to have The Conversation before you get together. It's certainly not easy, but if you know you're going to walk away upset if feelings aren't mutual, then you need to make that clear. When I met Laurie, she kept going on about how she didn't want a serious relationship; she just wanted to date a few guys and have fun. I took her at her word, and after our first kiss one night I didn't press for anything more. She started acting all sad and pouty, and I had no clue why! Turns out she'd only said that stuff because she didn't want to "scare me," but she actually was dying to go out with me. Sadly, it was too late. I'd already met another girl who was honest from the start, and I'd let myself start falling for her.

Laurie wasn't completely off base in her fear. If the instant you meet the guy, you start planning your wedding, trust me—he will run screaming. But Laurie took things too far. Don't lie about what you want. If you're looking for a relationship (someday in the future, after you know each other better, of course), then don't hide that fact.

And sometimes, no matter what you do or say, things won't work out. And all you can do is realize that it's probably not your fault and try to move on.

### Fun with Friends

Ah, the old to-date-a-friend-or-not-to-date-a-friend question. Will this one ever have a good answer? I'm not sure. With friends there's not as much game playing and awkwardness. You both know what you're getting into, and you already have a level of trust—the most important element. But is this enough?

It was for Craig and Leah. They were friends for years before they started going out. They lived on the same street, rode the bus together, even costarred in the school musical. Then on a class trip one time Craig's friends started teasing him about Leah. It's obvious you like her, they told him. You guys do everything together. How come you've never asked her out?

For some reason, it took that question for everything to click into place in Craig's head. Why hadn't he asked Leah out? She was perfect for him! But Craig had a ton of doubts. Leah was his best friend. If they dated and things went bad, would he lose her friendship?

When Craig got home from the trip, he called her, stumbling nervously through an admission of what he'd realized.

Leah was totally shocked but confessed that she'd thought about it, too. They made a deal to go for it but agreed that as soon as it seemed like it wasn't working, they'd go back to being friends.

At first, Craig told me, things were actually kind of strange. They had joked about other couples before, and now they were one! But then again, in a lot of ways it wasn't much different from what they had before, only more intense. They were still friends but also close in a new, exciting way.

To make this point for the millionth time, it takes a while for us to get comfortable with you—and especially with the idea of being in a relationship with you. So when we start out as friends, a lot of the anxiety is gone because you already know a lot of those deep, dark secrets. We don't have to prove our "manliness" to you on the field or act like nothing could possibly shake us. That means once we make that transition from friendship to more, things will probably be able to progress more quickly than they usually do. We might be more comfortable with being your "boyfriend" because all the scary stuff is out of the way.

## Friendly Fire

Now for the bad news. In Craig and Leah's case, things went great. And for all the reasons I just explained, there are many times when we'll be totally cool with dating a friend. But that doesn't mean it always works.

The downside to already being so comfortable with you is that it takes away a little of the thrill of dating. It's like seeing the end of a horror movie first, then watching the beginning and pretending you don't know who the killer will turn out to be. It's just tough to fake that early phase. That's why, as I said above, when relationships between friends do work out, they pretty much skip that part. But some guys (and girls—be honest!) think that tense, getting-to-know-you time is the best part.

"Once I'm good friends with a girl, I can't think of her like that," insists John, 16. "Part of what attracts me to a girl is that mystery thing, the fact that I don't know much about her. It's so much more fun getting to know someone when you're not really sure what they think of you and when you can't wait to kiss them."

My advice here, again, is probably not what you want to hear. There isn't any way to know for sure whether it's better to start out as friends or not. Sometimes the spark will be there, and sometimes it won't. But at least you might understand a little better why some guys are okay with it when some guys aren't. And one more thing I can tell you: Craig and Leah were being a little naive when they made the promise to stay friends no matter what. It's not always possible.

After only a few weeks of dating, Peter and Lily decided that they definitely made better friends than boyfriend and girlfriend. But suddenly they couldn't hang out together anymore. It felt strange and even stranger when Lily started dating someone else. Sometimes there's a point of no return that's hard to come back from, no matter how solid your friendship was before. This isn't true for everyone, but since it can happen—it's a good idea to wait to make the leap until you're both confident it's what you want.

## It Takes Time. . . .

This just can't be emphasized enough—we take a long time to open up. Please don't get frustrated with us if it's early in the relationship and we're not spilling our guts to you. If you're patient, I promise it will happen. We're kind of like those colored 3-D posters, with thousands of tiny dots—if you stare at them long enough, a cool picture emerges that's worth the wait.

It's not just that we don't want to get hurt. I'll come clean—we're very stubborn. We all know we're supposed to give things up to make a relationship work. But we're not too good at that whole compromise thing. Rocky Road ice cream lovers will rarely switch over to strawberry, and guys who are used to spending Friday nights with their friends may have trouble spending them on dates with you. But give him a little time to adjust, some gentle pushing, and he'll come around.

In general, you seem to get used to the idea of having a boyfriend much faster than we can shift ourselves into boyfriend mode. So if we act uncomfortable at first, it's just because we're slow learners. Work with us!

## The PDA Factor

We know many of you want us to be affectionate—to hold your hand as we walk down the hallway, kiss you at your locker, or hug you whenever and wherever if you're in a bad mood. But the truth is, some of us are not always comfortable with public displays of affection (aka PDA).

Why not?

Probably for the same reasons that some of you feel shy about it. But one bigger problem for guys is that a kiss in the spotlight can lead to hours of teasing from our friends. As I've already explained, there's a lot of pressure on us to look "in control" in front of other guys. When we hold your hand or kiss you, it sends out the opposite signal. On top of this, we still have the problem of not wanting our emotions to be on display for the world to see.

"My girlfriend Nicole thought I was ashamed of her because I didn't like to touch her around other people," Joel, 17, told me. "That wasn't true at all. It's just that my family's never been really touchy-feely, so it's hard for me to act like that with Nicole. When we're alone, it's one thing. But in front of our friends? Isn't that stuff supposed to be private, just between the two of us?"

Joel managed to convince Nicole that he was actually proud to have her as his girlfriend, but she still wanted him to be a little more affectionate with her. They decided to break him into the world of PDA slowly, starting with holding hands in a mall full of strangers before trying it out in front of their friends. It worked! Now Joel can give Nicole a hug or grab her hand in public without a problem. And it turned out that Nicole didn't really like kissing in public, either. So she and Joel agreed to keep it reserved for their alone time.

It's not that we're hopeless in the affection category—we're just not used to having our deepest feelings exposed to everyone around us. If your boyfriend has the same problem as Joel and you're interested in being more affectionate in public, try working out a compromise like the one Joel found with Nicole. As long as you're clear on the fact that your guy's hesitation has nothing to do with how much you mean to him, then it's worth being patient and making the extra effort.

## ENDGAME

Relationships end. Why? For a billion different reasons. Sometimes it's your choice, and sometimes it's ours. But I know a lot of you spend many hours agonizing over what made us call it quits, especially since guys tend not to explain themselves as much. I can't tell you what made your boyfriend break up with you, obviously, but I can give you some of the biggest reasons that guys generally feel the need to get out.

First of all, friends can play a huge role. We care a lot about what our friends think of us and the girls we're going out with. It's really lame, I know, but sometimes a guy whose friends are on his case about you all the time will break up with you just to make things normal again with them. He's tired of being picked on, or he figures that they know him well enough that he should trust their judgment anyway. This guy isn't worthy of you—he should be able to make his decisions on his own. But if your boyfriend's friends were always giving you both a hard time over the relationship and then he breaks up with you, it's a distinct possibility that there's a connection.

Sometimes even when our friends think you're great, they can still be an obstacle. When Danny, 16, started going out with Phoebe, none of his other guy friends had girlfriends. They would all hang out without him, and he kept feeling like he was missing out on something. He liked Phoebe a lot, but every time his friends would sit around the lunch table on Monday, talking about the stuff they'd done that weekend, he'd feel really left out. Danny finally broke up with Phoebe, and then after a few "guy" nights he got bored. He tried to get Phoebe back, but she wouldn't go for it. The crazy part is that Danny's friends later told him that they'd been so jealous of him the whole time he was with Phoebe. Any of them would have traded places with him in a second.

One way to possibly avoid this trap is to be understanding when your boyfriend wants to spend more time with his friends. If Danny had just gotten the male bonding ritual out of his system before breaking up with Phoebe, he would have realized sooner that he was being an idiot and he never would have dumped her. This doesn't mean you should sit back and let the guy control everything about when you see each other. Just make it clear that it's fine if sometimes you both do your own thing. If you two are always together, you probably miss your friends, too!

One of the most common causes of breakups is the all-painful "someone new" syndrome. There's very little chance he'll admit it to you, even when you call him on it, but if a guy you've been getting along with really well suddenly starts to withdraw, then breaks up with you, it could be because he met someone he likes better. It's not that there's anything wrong with you—it's just that this girl might seem even more right for him.

Adam, 15, had been dating Becky for a couple of months when he met Amanda. "Becky was really cool," he told me. "But Amanda and I just clicked right away."

Still, feeling guilty, Adam stayed with Becky and didn't tell her anything about Amanda. "I never cheated," Adam swears. But he did spend a lot of time on the phone with Amanda, and they once stayed up all night instant messaging each other. Meanwhile Becky started commenting on how different he acted with her. Every time she'd beg him to tell her what was wrong, he'd brush her off, acting angry at her for asking when really he was angry at himself for lying. (Note—if a guy reacts this defensively when you know you're asking valid questions, then there's a good chance you're on to something. We typically lash out at someone else when the real person we're upset with is ourselves.)

Eventually Adam realized that he couldn't keep pretending. He was falling hard for Amanda, and he still cared enough about Becky that he hated hurting her. "It was tough because I knew Becky and I wouldn't last," Adam told me, "but I didn't know how to let her know that." So what did he end up doing? He broke up with Becky over the phone, never mentioning Amanda or even giving a specific reason. Soon afterward he and Amanda became a couple.

These are just a few of the reasons why things sometimes don't work out. A lot of the time it's just that as we get to know each other better, we realize that we don't have as much in common as we thought. There's no definite answer here, but trust your instincts and remember that you'll be happier without this guy in the long run, anyway.

### Nothing but the Truth

Now you know a little more about why we end things, but you're still probably wondering how we manage to do it in such totally lame ways—like Adam's botched attempt with Becky, where he never came clean. No one likes having to hurt someone, especially someone you cared about enough to go out with in the first place. And one of the scariest things to us, right up there with death and being creamed on the basketball court, is watching you cry. We will go to great, absolutely ridiculous lengths to avoid it.

This explains the phone breakup, the answering machine breakup, and even the (ouch) e-mail breakup. It's also why it can often be so hard to pin us down on a reason. We're trying to make this experience as fast as possible, and in our twisted logic we feel that the less we have to explain, the sooner we're gone and out of range of your potential tears. Also, being the (just slightly) less emotionally mature gender, we might not even know how to put the reason into words. We're not as good at that "communicating" thing as you are. We don't have as much practice. So we're afraid that if we try, it could come out sounding worse than it does in our heads, and we'll only hurt you more—or give you reason to believe there's still a chance, when there isn't.

Don't assume that because a guy dumps you in a jerky way it means he never cared about you. Actually, it can really mean the exact opposite. He did and probably still does care and—as I said—just can't stand to see you upset. This is also the explanation behind the old "make her break up with me" routine. You know, the one where he keeps avoiding you and not returning your calls until you finally cut things off first.

I'm not trying to win your sympathy here. I know it's awful to be treated this way, and there are times when the reality is that we're wimps or just plain lazy and trying to make you do all the work. But I do want you to understand that there's usually a lot more going on than you might realize at first. I know girls think that we can walk away like it was nothing, that we're not feeling nearly as much as you are just because we don't act like it in front of you.

Not true. Whichever one of us is doing the dumping, we still feel bad about the whole thing—we just can't express it as well as you can. It is, after all, a difficult thing to say. So keep that in mind the next time you decide that all guys are creeps because someone broke up with you in a lousy way. We're not all bad. I promise.

## THE RULES

So what about when it's you in the hot seat? Ever wish you could know the best way to break a guy's heart without, well, breaking his heart? Below are some ground rules guys secretly wish girls would follow when ending it . . . the stuff nobody talks about:

BREAK UP IN PERSON. I know, I just finished explaining that most of us guys have trouble doing this. But that doesn't mean we can't at least try. In the end, it's better for both of us to have concrete, solid answers spelled out. The only way to make the truth hit home with us is to tell us to our faces that we are definitely through.

PRETEND TO GIVE US A CHANCE TO TALK YOU OUT OF IT. We like to be right. So, we may try to passionately convince you breaking up is a bad idea. Deep down we probably know it's pointless, but we need to tell ourselves we tried or else we'll really feel like losers. Hearing the guy out, even if you've made up your mind, is a totally stellar thing to do.

GIVE US SOME SPACE. Running into somebody after a breakup can be a nightmare. And the last thing we want is for you to see how much you've really hurt us. Remember the fragile male ego I keep mentioning? It's all over if you catch sight of the pain in our eyes. A lot of times girls think the nicest thing to do is to keep being friendly after the breakup, to act like you still care. You know what? Steer clear of us, at least for a little while, until the wound has a chance to start healing. Then maybe—maybe—we can start to be friends.

RERUN

It happens all the time. Just when you think it's over, it's not. And sometimes you actually need the breakup to see how much you mean to each other.

After I'd been dating Meg for about five months, we got in this big blowout fight and decided to end it. I was miserable. I thought about her ten times a day and twenty times a night. Not only did I miss her, but I realized that what I'd said in that fight was wrong.

Meg and I had made a decision to stop talking completely. But at the end of the week I broke the rule and called her. I told her how I felt and how sorry I was. After a long talk we agreed to get back together.

Those first weeks after the breakup were amazing. I appreciated Meg so much more, and it was easier to ignore all the little things that used to get on my nerves.

So if you and your boyfriend reach a point where all you do is fight but you think that underneath it all you have something too special to give up on, maybe the best idea is to take time off. When you're not around each other all the time, what matters and what doesn't becomes so much clearer.

Then again, history repeats itself and repeats itself. My girlfriend Julie and I broke up nine times—I swear—and every time we thought that was it. But we would always come back together for all the wrong reasons because we missed having someone, not necessarily each other.

So here's one you don't even need me to tell you— make sure that if you do consider getting back together, you're doing it because he's the right guy for you.

## The Big Test

Many of us do try to stay friends with our exes, even though it sometimes seems like there's a better chance of discovering that the world really is flat. The trick, as you probably know, is to wait a while to let the hurt feelings cool down.

Bill, 16, isn't the kind of guy to hold grudges. And he brags that he's still good friends with every girl he's ever dated. But Bill's personal rule is a two-week time-out after the relationship ends. My friend Greg agrees.

"Nobody likes getting dumped," Greg says, "but at least for me, it's more than just the hurt of losing the girl. I have a lot on the line, and I tend to take breakups as a real failure."

Once we do work through these feelings and manage to become friends with you, a whole new complication enters the picture. What if one of us starts to fall for the other's friends?

## Ex Plus Ex Equals . . . ?

It's not that hard to end up in one of these triangles. You're just a bud now, not a girlfriend. You're hanging around us and probably around our friends, and they no longer look at you as off-limits in that same way.

Before you even consider going for it, ask yourself a couple of questions. How much time has passed since the end of your relationship with the first guy? If it was a recent thing, it's not a good idea. He may act like he's over it, but trust me—he's not. When my friend Mark's ex Kathy got together with his friend Nick just a month after Mark and Kathy's breakup, Mark was wrecked. But you wouldn't have guessed it from looking at the big grin he flashed whenever they were around. He also swore up and down to Kathy that he couldn't care less. Remember—we will do anything we can to hide our insecurities from you.

More questions: Most important—how serious was your relationship with him? How long were you with him in the first place? How close is he to the particular friend you've got your eye on? Also, is he dating someone else yet? If he is, that gives you a big green light.

If you've been over all this in your head and everything's adding up to the right answer (you didn't date guy number one for long, it wasn't too serious, it's a casual friend of his, etc. . . .), then things look promising. But you should still know that some guys, no matter what, will not be psyched about this situation.

Of course, Brett, 15, makes the point that it can be hard among his group not to date ex-girlfriends. He says that everyone in his clique ends up dating one another, and no one really minds because it's so common. Brett and Samantha went out for two months, and after they broke up (Brett dumped Samantha), Samantha said it would take her years to date again. Two weeks later she was going out with Brett's best friend, Paul.

Samantha obviously got over it pretty quickly. Did Brett mind? Actually, no. By that time he was dating Shelly, another girl from their group. He and Shelly were so into each other, he said he didn't care that Samantha and Paul were together. If we like our new crush enough, we can bounce back much more easily.

Overall, it's a good idea to avoid dating an ex's friend, but if it does happen, remember to be considerate. Don't flaunt your new relationship in the guy's face, and let his friend be the one to tell him. Respect their friendship and be careful not to try to turn either one against the other or put them in the middle of fights. Keep your relationship with the friend totally separate from whatever happened with the first guy. That way there's a chance you could come out of this with all of your friendships intact. That would sure be something, wouldn't it?

# CHAPTER FIVE:

# WHAT YOU DIDN'T KNOW YOU NEVER KNEW

WELL, YOU'VE LISTENED TO ME THIS FAR.

YOU DESERVE SOME KIND OF REWARD

FOR THAT. HOW ABOUT IF I LET YOU IN

ON THE STUFF THAT'S SO WEIRD, SO RAN-

DOM, OR SO PERSONAL, WE RARELY

EVEN TELL OUR CLOSEST GIRL FRIENDS? A

LOT OF GUYS OUT THERE WON'T LIKE WHAT

I'M DOING HERE, BUT YOU'LL STICK UP

FOR ME, RIGHT? RIGHT?

## WORD GAMES

"Don't be a Ricci," my friends like to say when one of us is acting really lame. Don't bother looking "Ricci" up in a dictionary—you won't find it. See, there's this guy Ricci we went to school with, and he was always bugging everyone about stupid, pointless stuff.

"Man, it's pretty hot out," we used to say on the coldest winter days. And no, we didn't have inhumanly warm blood in our veins. It was just another in-joke— saying the opposite of what we really meant. We use these little "codes" (made-up words based on people's names, sarcastic lines, etc.) as a way to communicate with our friends. The guys you know probably have similar weird expressions they've started to use over time—things that wouldn't make sense to anyone outside of the group.

In general, we aren't as talkative as you are. So we don't necessarily "bond" with our friends through sharing lots of words and feelings. Instead we have certain words that we feel cool using—words that an outsider can't figure out right away. This doesn't mean we walk around communicating in foreign languages or anything. We just throw these words or phrases into our conversations as a way to make each other laugh or remind each other of thoughts and ideas we have in common. So the next time you hear your boyfriend on the phone with a friend, talking about how "Crofty" the movie you just saw was, don't worry that you're not prepared enough for the SATs. It's probably just another one of "their" words.

## Calling It Off

We do not fear phones as much as you think we do. Actually, we don't fear them at all. They're great for certain purposes, such as deciding the exact time we're supposed to meet for the movie or finding out how your big bio test went. But calling just to . . . talk? Where's the point? Isn't that a waste of time? There are so many things we could be doing right now!

We like to be active, to be constantly moving toward an accomplishment. When we end a phone call with you after what feels to you like a short time, it doesn't mean we don't like you. It's just that some guys get bored on the phone—bored and restless. Sometimes, when there's nothing else going on, we'll stay on the phone for longer, especially if there's actually a lot to talk about. And I do have a few guy friends who can outlast their girlfriends on the phone. But for many of us, those long rambling calls about nothing give us the itch to hang up and go shoot a few hoops or something.

I bet you've got lots of girlfriends who are up for

those intense, marathon phone sessions. So next time you're in the mood, maybe try one of them. We'll be fine with that. Just don't forget to give us a quick buzz first and set up plans to go out later!

## Boys Do Cry

Yes, it happens, though rarely in front of anyone—especially you. It's not an easy thing to fake (and why would we want to, anyway, with all that pressure on us not to do it?), so if you actually witness it happening, take the guy seriously.

Of course, if you don't see your boyfriend cry at a time when you'd expect him to, like when you're about to go away for the summer or something, don't take it as an insult. It doesn't mean he doesn't care or even that he's holding something back. We're told over and over how "unmanly" it is to cry, so some guys take that training to heart until it reaches a point where they can't cry even when they want to. It's tough to overcome years of brainwashing. You know how sick you are of feeling like you need to look like those models in the magazines (even though we don't want you to)? That's how it is for us with crying.

When the tears do start flowing, be supportive, but don't overdo it to the point where he'll just be embarrassed. If you ever want to see him this vulnerable

# FIVE THINGS YOU NEVER GUESSED MIGHT MAKE US CRY

1. The death of a pet
2. Certain sad movies—especially if they involve baseball, like *Field of Dreams*
3. Breakups
4. Winning or losing a major sports game
5. The death of a sports hero or a favorite musician

again, act like it's no big deal (not whatever's got him crying, obviously, but the fact that he reacted this way). Let him know you're there if he needs it, to listen or give him a hug, but you can also just be there while he cries it out of his system. The first time I cried in front of my girlfriend Tara, she freaked out, as if I was dying or something. She made it seem like seeing me cry was such a huge deal, and even though she was trying to be nice (rushing madly around searching for tissues, widening her eyes in sympathy, etc.), I never felt comfortable crying around her again.

Another thing: If you've watched us cry and lived to tell, don't. Tell, that is. See, there's another reason I never cried in front of Tara after that first time. Later that night, at dinner with a group of friends, my buddy Rick started teasing me about being Mr. Insensitivity because of something stupid I said. Tara leaped to my "defense" by announcing to a table full of guys that I'd been "bawling" just a few hours ago. See—he is sensitive, she explained. I'll leave it to your imaginations what followed afterward, once I was alone with the guys. And for months and months to come, too.

## The Green Monster

Even the most cool, confident guy (which, as you're probably figuring out, is usually a front, anyway) sometimes has a problem with jealousy. It's one of our biggest weaknesses, but there is a way to fight it—and you can help.

My friend David thought his girlfriend Colleen flirted too much. It drove him crazy. He would watch her laugh with all her guy friends, leaning up against them and touching them in casual but affectionate ways. He believed her when she said they were just friends but still wished she would be a little more distant.

David never told Colleen what he was thinking, but he did confide in his friends. One day one of his friends let out the secret to Colleen. Instead of freaking out, Colleen kept cool. She was hurt that he would worry about her ever cheating on him but realized that going off on him about his insecurities would only make things worse. (Go, Colleen!) She found a way to bring up the topic in a natural-seeming way and coaxed him into admitting his fears. She reassured him as firmly as possible that he had nothing to worry about, asking for specific behaviors that were upsetting him and explaining what those incidences were really about.

David felt much better after the conversation, especially when Colleen made more of an effort to include David when she hung out with her guy friends. This made him feel more secure. She still hung out with the guys, which David knew she had every right to do, but she was more sensitive to David's feelings.

Of course, there will always be guys who are mad with jealousy even when you tell them outright they have nothing to worry about. If your boyfriend won't let up on the topic, it's probably time to ask for some space. Then hopefully he'll figure out he needs to accept you as you are if he wants you in his life.

The rest of us just need a little propping up once in a while to remind us that you're all ours. Even if a guy tells you he feels no jealousy, he probably does. It's hard for us not to. So any way you can boost his confidence in your commitment to him can't hurt. And he should be doing the same for you!

"OPRAH" TIME

Ask a guy if he's in touch with his "feminine side," and he will probably give you a funny look and run away. But ask him some specific questions, and he will be forced to answer yes. Here are some common myths about us demythified for you:

MYTH: Guys don't care how they look.
REALITY: Do you have any idea how much time we spend accomplishing that casual, "don't-care" look? Plenty of us use gel, mousse, or other products in our hair. I've been known to change my clothes no less than eight times before a big date. We primp. We preen. Some of us have even tried to diet or work out like crazy to build up our muscles. We worry all the time about our appearances, and we do everything we can to look good, but we're just not allowed to admit it the way you are.

MYTH: Girls like animals more than guys do.
REALITY: Have you ever seen a guy with his dog? When we're alone with our pets, we get more emotional and cutesy than you'd probably want to see. Sure, we tend to be more aggressive with the animals—there's a lot more belly scratching and play fighting. But that's how we, along with our pets, express affection! Maybe

it's because animals don't need us to talk and spill our souls to them, but they still form attachments to us that won't break no matter what we do. Our relationships with pets are where we learn how to care, and the toughest, hardest guy can be reduced to Mr. Vulnerable when he's alone with his puppy.

MYTH: You won't find stuffed animals or childhood toys in guys' bedrooms.

REALITY: Your boyfriend might not admit it, but when he was younger, he had at least one toy or comfort object you couldn't pry from him with a crowbar. For me it was a yellow wool blanket. I slept with it so much that I wore a hole right through it. By the time I was four, all that was left was the fringe. At that point my parents took it away because they were afraid I would strangle myself in my sleep. No matter how much I cried, they wouldn't give it back.

Chances are things like blankets and teddy bears haven't traveled that far. Most end up on closet shelves or bookcases, usually within easy reach. It's sort of a security measure, like one of those fire axes in a glass case. We know we can break in and get it in case of an emergency, even though we never do. But it's always good to know it's there.

# THE
# CONCLUSION?

We know we have issues. We get a little too caught up in our own worlds sometimes, we have trouble saying everything we feel, and we can be pretty tough to figure out. But come on—no one's perfect, and at least we're trying! Maybe now that you know a little more about why we are the way we are, it will make things easier. Because deep down we all want the same thing—to be understood and liked, quirks and all.

We've told you our secrets. Now it's time for you to return the favor and come clean about yours. . . .